There was no way to close the box now. . . .

Inside, almost filling it, was what looked more than anything else like a kind of propeller. It had four oddly shaped, curving blades, one pointing directly at each corner of the box. The blades were a couple of inches below the top of the box. In the center of the blades was a kind of dial, like a round combination lock. But instead of numbers, around the dial were funny-looking symbols, sort of like hieroglyphics.

Things that looked like thorns or roots, gnarled and twisting and branching, clung to the inside surfaces of the metal box.

I didn't like it. I didn't like it at all. I especially didn't like it that I couldn't close it. . . .

"Sleator's use of language and his creation of characters, both human and alien, are captivating."

—*Children's Literature*

PUFFIN BOOKS BY WILLIAM SLEATOR

The Beasties
The Boxes
The Boy Who Reversed Himself
Dangerous Wishes
The Duplicate
The Green Futures of Tycho
House of Stairs
Interstellar Pig
Into the Dream
The Night the Heads Came
Oddballs
Others See Us
Singularity
The Spirit House
Strange Attractors

WILLIAM SLEATOR

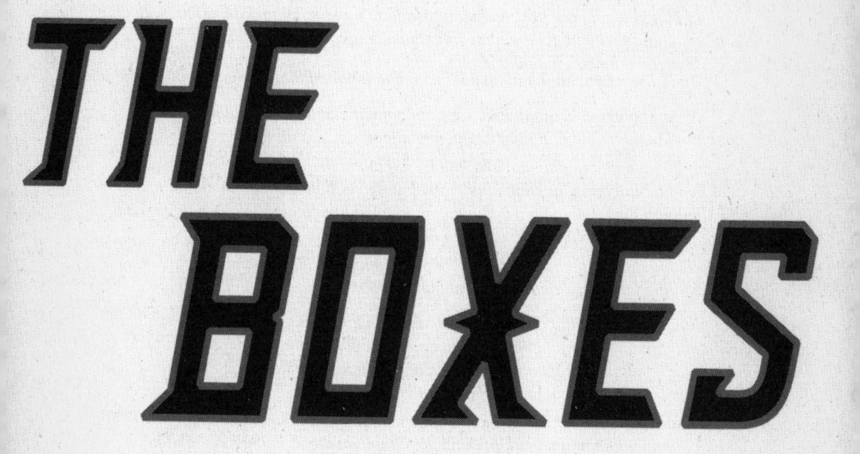

PUFFIN BOOKS

The author would like to thank Paul Curtis,
architect, for his information about real-estate procedures,
which helped a great deal with the plot.

PUFFIN BOOKS
Published by the Penguin Group
Penguin Putnam Books for Young Readers,
345 Hudson Street, New York, New York 10014, U.S.A.
Penguin Books Ltd, 27 Wrights Lane, London W8 5TZ, England
Penguin Books Australia Ltd, Ringwood, Victoria, Australia
Penguin Books Canada Ltd, 10 Alcorn Avenue, Toronto, Ontario, Canada M4V 3B2
Penguin Books (N.Z.) Ltd, 182-190 Wairau Road, Auckland 10, New Zealand

Penguin Books Ltd, Registered Offices: Harmondsworth, Middlesex, England

First published in the United States of America by Dutton Children's Books,
a member of Penguin Putnam Inc., 1998
Published by Puffin Books,
a division of Penguin Putnam Books for Young Readers, 2000

5 7 9 10 8 6 4

THE LIBRARY OF CONGRESS HAS CATALOGED THE DUTTON EDITION AS FOLLOWS:
Sleator, William.
The boxes / by William Sleator.—1st ed.
p. cm.
Summary: When she opens two strange boxes left in her care by her mysterious
uncle, fifteen-year-old Annie discovers a swarm of telepathic creatures
and unleashes a power capable of slowing down time.
ISBN 0-525-46012-8 (hc)
[1. Science fiction.] I. Title.
PZ7.S63138Bn 1998 [Fic]—dc21 98-9285 CIP AC

Puffin Books ISBN 0-14-130810-9

Printed in the United States of America

For my father,

WILLIAM WARNER SLEATOR, JR.,

whose example of thoughtful calmness in almost any crisis has helped to keep me from being more of a nervous wreck than I already am

THE BOXES

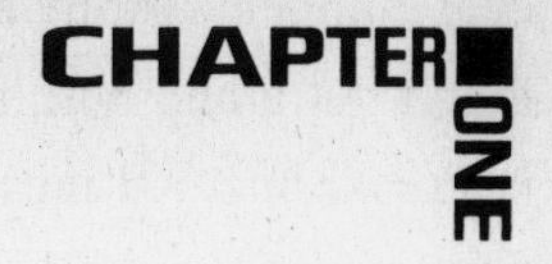

"And *don't* try to open them. Don't even *think* about trying to open them," Uncle Marco said. "I'm leaving them with you because you're the only person here I can trust. No one else can know they even exist."

"What about Aunt Ruth?" I asked him. Aunt Ruth was my legal guardian; I lived in her house. My Uncle Marco did, too, when he was around, which was almost never.

Uncle Marco's face hardened. "*Especially* not Ruth!" he said, his voice so uncharacteristically serious it was a little jolting. "That would be about the worst thing that could ever happen." Aunt Ruth was his younger sister, but he didn't get along with her any better than I did.

"Yeah, but . . . I mean, this is her house. If you're leaving your boxes here with me, she could find them. Wouldn't it be safer to put them in a bank vault or something? What's in them, anyway?"

Uncle Marco pushed back his thick black hair. He had a narrow face with a strong nose and a cleft chin, and pale blue eyes. He was very good-looking. "First of all, Annie, they're not *my* boxes," he said. "They can't belong to anybody; they just have to be guarded. And I don't trust banks. All they care about is making money. Who could ever trust somebody like that? *Ruth* works in a bank! You're ingenious enough to keep the boxes hidden." He frowned in concentration. "Of course, they can't be in the same place; they can't be anywhere near each other. Your room ought to be pretty safe for one of them—it's too much of a mess for anybody to find anything there. The other one can go in the basement. Ruth never goes down there. She's terrified of the basement." He moved his lips into a thin smile. "I made sure she was from the year one."

"She never does go down there," I said, thinking about it. "But why did you want her to be afraid of the basement? What did you do to frighten—"

"We better hurry," he said, not answering me. "It's five o'clock. She'll be home from work soon. Let's move the boxes now."

Uncle Marco was always doing that, dropping some intriguing hint about something and then never explaining what he meant. He played with my curiosity. He was the same way about the places he was traveling to all the time. He would never say exactly where he was going, just that it was really important for him to be there right away.

"Is your uncle ever going to grow up and settle down?" Aunt Ruth would say disapprovingly whenever he was about to leave, which was always only a few days after he got back from the last place. Aunt Ruth was as critical of Uncle Marco as she was of me. Even though he was her older brother, she couldn't stop telling me what he should do. The funny thing was, he *looked* so much younger than Aunt Ruth, even though she was forty-five and he was fifty. When I asked him about it privately, all he would say was that her rotten disposition had prematurely aged her. But she wasn't prematurely aged; it was Uncle Marco who looked uncannily young.

Did I ever wish it was Uncle Marco who stayed at home and Aunt Ruth who was always away!

I'd been wishing this as long as I could remember. I never knew my parents; they died in an accident when I was an infant. My mother was the middle child. Even fifteen years ago, when the accident happened, Uncle Marco was already in the mysterious habit of traveling all the time, while Aunt Ruth had a steady job and was living in the old house our family had owned for generations. It only made sense for me to stay with her, in the eyes of the lawyers and the courts, and she went along with it. She'd had no choice, she was always telling me as soon as I was old enough to understand. She had sacrificed her life and a lot of her money for my sake—and if I didn't start getting better grades or making more friends, she'd take me to the orphanage where I belonged.

This always made me feel horribly guilty. It was Uncle Marco who told me, when I was around ten, that Aunt Ruth really had it easy, and I hadn't been any trouble for her at all. She had a free place to live; she had plenty of money even aside from her job at the bank; she could easily have afforded to hire nurses to take care of me when I was young, or day care when I was a little older. After I understood that, I didn't feel as guilty. But I didn't like Aunt Ruth any better. And no matter what, there didn't seem to be anything I could do to get her to like me.

If it hadn't been for Uncle Marco's visits, I don't know what I would have done. It was Uncle Marco who comforted me, who listened to me, who understood me. He was the closest thing to a real parent I had, even though he was away so much. Sometimes I would beg him to take me with him. He said I was still too young—what he was doing was too important and too dangerous for him to put me at risk. After I was grown up—if I turned out to be a decent and trustworthy and independent person—then maybe he could make me his partner. Partner in *what*? I would ask. But he would never say.

Anyway, Aunt Ruth and the authorities would never have let him take me.

Now Uncle Marco pulled one box from out of his closet and the other from under his bed. He tore off the brown paper wrapping with his name and our address neatly printed on it in black marker. There was also a strange mark stamped on the paper in blue ink, something like a Chinese character. I wanted to ask him about it, but he didn't give me a chance. "Okay. Which one do you want in your room, which one in the basement?" he asked me as we studied the two objects in his sparsely furnished, unlived-in bedroom.

"But what's in them?" I asked.

He shook his head. "No time for that now, Annie. You've got to decide which one goes where."

They were both the same size, cubes about a foot and a half on a side. One was wooden, like a simple crate, but with no gaps or cracks between the strips of wood. The other was dark gray, made out of some kind of metal, dented, stained, and corroded, as though it had been around for a very long time. Neither had what looked like a lid or a keyhole or any other visible means of being opened.

"It looks like there's no way to open them, no matter how hard you try," I murmured.

"That's right," he said brusquely. "They can't be opened, period. Which one goes where?"

"Did they let you carry them both on the plane, or did you have to check them?" I asked. I had never been on an airplane—Aunt Ruth said she couldn't afford to give me undeserved luxuries like that—but I had read and heard enough about traveling to know about carry-ons and checked bags.

"Check them?" Uncle Marco said, sounding a little confused. "You mean . . . Oh, of course. No, I didn't check them! I couldn't let anybody else handle them or risk losing them. Of course I, uh, carried them on."

"They seem a little big to fit under the seat or—"

He looked at his watch. "We've got to hurry. Which one goes where?"

The wooden one looked like it belonged in a basement; the metal one looked too heavy to carry very far. "Let's take the wooden one down to the basement and put the other one in my room," I said.

Uncle Marco watched me from under his dark eyebrows. "You're sure about that?"

"Why not?" I said, feeling uncomfortable now. "Is there something wrong with doing it that way? What difference does it make if I can't open them anyway?"

"I just wanted you to be sure. Once we've put them there, you won't be able to move them on your own. Let's go."

They were both surprisingly heavy, and Uncle Marco took most of the weight. He was tall, and though he was slender, you could tell he was strong. He was wearing a black sleeveless sweater and a shirt of some ethnic woven material in blue, red, and purple. The sleeves were rolled up above his elbows, and veins and muscles stood out on his bare forearms as we maneuvered the wooden box down two flights of stairs. Again, I wondered how in the world he had carried both boxes onto the plane.

We put the wooden box in a far corner of the dark, smelly basement, hiding it behind some cardboard boxes. Uncle Marco brushed off his hands. Then he paused, thinking. "Is that development company still bugging Ruth about wanting to buy the house?" he said, looking back at where we put the box.

"Yeah, they are," I said, a little out of breath. "They're pressuring everybody in the neighborhood to sign away their houses soon so they can tear them down and build a giant mall. But Aunt Ruth swears she'll never give in."

"That's good." He sounded relieved. "Nobody's as stubborn as Ruth! If she says she won't sell, we're safe."

"Safe?" I asked him as we started up the stairs. "What do you mean, safe? What does selling the house have to do with the boxes?"

"Nothing, nothing." He waved my question aside. "I was just curious, that's all."

Up in my room, we moved some junk out of my closet, put the metal box in there, then covered it with the junk. We were just finishing when we heard Aunt Ruth slam the front door at 5:31.

"Act normal, Annie. Do what you normally do when she gets home from work," Uncle Marco told me.

So I stayed in my room and Uncle Marco went back to his.

Aunt Ruth didn't call out a greeting or anything; she

turned on the TV. She'd be glued to it until dinnertime. She never bothered much about cooking; she would just open cans or thaw something. Sometimes I made recipes myself, and they weren't bad—Aunt Ruth ate the food, all right. But she would tell me I was wasting my time messing up the kitchen when I should be studying.

She told me to tell Uncle Marco he was wasting his time when he cooked, too, but he ignored her. Uncle Marco loved to cook and always made exotic and delicious food when he was home. He and I had had fun cooking together earlier, before he told me about the boxes. We had made a wonderful concoction of rice and sausage and seafood and vegetables, hearty and spicy, with different condiments to sprinkle on it. Now we went downstairs and heated it up. Aunt Ruth ate about twice as much as either of us. She didn't like to cook, but she *did* like to eat. She had gained so much weight recently that she was starting to waddle, and her face was puffy. It didn't help that her frizzy hair was rapidly turning gray.

Uncle Marco, ten years older, had an unlined face and perfectly black hair. He looked about twenty-five.

"Anne, ask your uncle where he's off to next," she told me when she had stopped shoveling in the food—she always refused to address Uncle Marco directly. "Oh, sorry," she added. "I didn't mean you to ask him *where* he's going; I know he would never tell *me* that. I meant to ask *when* he is taking off next."

"When, Uncle Marco?" I asked him, dreading the answer.

"Tell your aunt it's the day after tomorrow, I'm afraid," he said, looking sadly at me, as though he felt guilty for deserting me.

Aunt Ruth caught the glance. "Are you and your uncle hiding something from me?" she demanded, starting to get angry.

I turned to him.

"Why would I hide anything from my dear little sister?" Uncle Marco said smoothly.

"He's not hiding anything," I lied to Aunt Ruth.

Aunt Ruth snorted, really mad now. "He hides his whole life from me, for starters," she said. "I know he's the oldest, but I'm the one with clout at the bank, and I'm the executor of Father's estate. Tell your uncle I could easily cut off his annuity and stop his gallivanting around for good. And I would if I felt he was turning you against me. You always were an ungrateful brat," she added routinely.

She had threatened to cut off his money before, but it still made Uncle Marco uncomfortable enough that he appealed to her directly. "Please don't be paranoid, Ruth," he said, sounding genuinely concerned. "Annie and I aren't hiding anything. We're good friends, that's all."

"It's just as well he's leaving the day after tomorrow," Aunt Ruth said to me, still refusing to respond to him. "I feel like an outsider in my own house when he's around. And it's not good for you to get used to having him here.

The longer he stays, the longer you go through your self-pitying, malingering mood after he's left." She stood up. "You and your uncle can clean up the mess you made—I've been working hard all day. I'm sure you'd love more time alone together to say nasty things about me anyway."

Uncle Marco and I didn't look at each other.

Aunt Ruth moved away from the table, then turned back. "And if you and your uncle *are* hiding something from me, you can bet I'll find out. And then"—she ran her finger across her throat—"no more annuity." She waddled over to the TV.

CHAPTER TWO

What was in the boxes?

At school the next day, Friday, I ate lunch with my best friends, Linda and Jeff. We usually ate together, though it wasn't only because they wanted my company. I was also kind of a screen. If they ate alone all the time, people would notice, and it could get back to their parents—and their parents absolutely did not want them to see each other at all. With me and sometimes others there, it wouldn't look like anything special was going on between them.

Today, Henry ate with us, too. Henry lived close to us

in the neighborhood, and he liked me. I knew I was O.K., looks-wise. I have short black hair and dark eyes and I'm in good shape. Henry's a nice guy, and good-looking, too. But I wasn't interested in Henry or in any other boys my age. There weren't any who were as smart or as fun or as mysterious or as handsome as Uncle Marco. Anyway, Aunt Ruth thought fifteen was too young to go out alone with a boy. We couldn't double-date with Linda and Jeff because nobody could know they ever went out. So that was my excuse for not going out with Henry. But he kept reminding me that he was waiting for my sixteenth birthday.

"Annie, I gotta tell you what happened last night," Henry said breathlessly as he sat down with his tray.

"Uh-huh," I said, not paying much attention. I was thinking about the boxes. Curiosity about them was driving me crazy.

Henry lowered his voice, though Linda and Jeff were giggling together and not paying any attention anyway. "Around nine o'clock I went out to walk Fifi—you know, our bloodhound."

"Mmm," I said, nodding vaguely. If I just took a little peek inside the boxes after Uncle Marco left, how would he ever know?

"And as soon as I got to the sidewalk, this car pulled away from the curb," Henry was saying. "I didn't think anything about it at first—until I began to notice the car was going really slow, like it was following me!" He stared at me, wide-eyed.

"Huh?" I said.

"This car was following me. Like it had been waiting there for me to come out."

"You sure you weren't imagining it?" I asked him, interested enough now to stop thinking about the boxes for a minute.

"Yes, I'm sure. It was going so slow and keeping right behind me. I felt . . . uncomfortable. I tried to make Fifi hurry so I could turn around and get back inside the house, but she took her time, as usual. I was sure glad she was with me and I wasn't alone, though. If it hadn't been for the dog, maybe they would . . ."

"Would what?"

He shrugged. "Oh, I don't know." He seemed embarrassed to confess what he had been afraid of. "It was just so weird, the way the car was kind of inching along right behind me. Like it was threatening me or something. Finally I pulled Fifi around and went back—and the car turned around in a driveway and stayed right behind me."

"That *is* weird," I admitted.

"And when I told Mom and Dad, they looked scared, too. They didn't say much, but I could tell what they were thinking: Crutchley Development."

"Crutchley? Really?"

Henry nodded grimly.

Crutchley Development was the big company that was on the verge of buying out the neighborhood to tear the old houses down and build a giant mall. They wanted our house and Henry's house, too. Henry's house was bigger and older than ours. But his family wasn't rich; his grandparents had bought the place a long time ago.

Henry's parents and Aunt Ruth were the last people in the neighborhood to hold out—Crutchley was paying more for the run-down houses than anybody else would. I was always talking to different people at Crutchley Development on the phone so Aunt Ruth wouldn't have to, and they were getting ruder and ruder. The neighborhood was close to the highway, which made it a good location for a mall.

"You think a big company like that would use, like, gangster tactics?" I said, doubtful but also uncomfortable myself. If they were targeting Henry, they might target me, too.

"No other tactics worked with us or with you either. And they really want the property. If they're going to do things like this, how are we going to protect ourselves? I don't want Mom and Dad or your aunt to give in, but if they thought we were in danger . . ."

Henry wasn't Uncle Marco, but he was probably the nicest boy I knew. I didn't like seeing him upset—and we were in this together. "They can't get away with it," I tried to reassure him. "Aunt Ruth practically runs the bank, for one thing. And if anything like that happens again, we should tell the cops."

"They'd probably just think I was being hysterical," he said.

The bell rang, to my relief. I was concerned about the developers—if Henry really *wasn't* imagining this—but I was more concerned about the boxes. I wanted to get back to dwelling on them in class.

"Maybe . . . maybe I could walk you home after school," Henry suggested.

"Not today, Henry. I've got to get home real fast today," I said. "Maybe next week."

"Sure. See you."

Of course I had to get home as soon as possible today because Uncle Marco was leaving tomorrow.

CHAPTER THREE

The Saturday Uncle Marco left was a miserably cold and bleak January day, with snow flurries in the air. In the winter, I always secretly prayed there would be a blizzard when he was supposed to go so that he would be delayed for a day or two or even a week. But oddly, no matter how bad the weather was, Uncle Marco's flights were never canceled. He would politely ask me to say good-bye to Aunt Ruth and hug me, then get into a taxi in his long woolen coat, carrying his old leather satchel. There was always a certain tension about him when he left. I couldn't tell whether he was excited or apprehensive or a mixture of both.

And Aunt Ruth was right; I always *was* depressed after he went away. Though I tried to hide it so she wouldn't get angry, it wasn't easy.

This time it was worse than usual. Uncle Marco put a finger to his lips as the cab was pulling away, not realizing that Aunt Ruth was watching, too.

"What was that all about?" Aunt Ruth demanded as I stepped inside. "It looked like he was telling you to keep quiet about something."

"I didn't notice anything," I said, pretending to wipe a speck of dust out of my eye.

Aunt Ruth glared at me. "You sure?" she said suspiciously. Then she sighed. "You know, it really bothers me the way you get so moody after that man leaves," she complained. "I'm the one who brought you up; I'm the one who took care of you like a mother. He couldn't have cared less about you. He was always away! It's easy for him to be fun and lovable when he's only here for a couple of days every few months." She lit a cigarette and blew smoke at me. "He didn't have to nurse you when you were sick, or make sure you did your homework, or buy clothes for you, or give you nourishing food every day. And yet you obviously adore him and barely tolerate me. It hurts, Anne; it really, really hurts."

"But it's not like that, Aunt Ruth. I really do appreciate everything you've done for me," I said.

"I don't appreciate that tone of voice. And I meant what I said the other night. If I find out you and that man are hiding anything from me, that's the end of his annuity. And to think what my life would have been like if I hadn't been burdened with you all these years!"

It would have been exactly the same, except you wouldn't have the pleasure of complaining about me, I thought. "I better go do some studying to make up for the last couple of days," I said. "Let me know if you need some help with anything."

"Well, I'm not going to spend a lot of time cooking, if that's what you're thinking," she said, "Unlike your precious uncle, I work five days a week, in case you didn't notice. I've earned the right to relax on a Saturday." She sank heavily down in front of the TV, her cigarettes and candy within easy reach.

I trudged up the big wooden staircase with the carved banister and the stained glass window on the landing, thinking about running away. I knew there were a lot of kids my age who had left home and were surviving somehow on the streets. Almost anything would be better than living with Aunt Ruth. Except it was so cold out there! And what would I do about money? Even at fifteen I didn't have anything like my own bank account. Aunt Ruth doled out the cash very stingily and only when I worked up the nerve to ask; I had never had a regular allowance. But the main reason I didn't run away was that if I did, I would miss Uncle Marco the next time he came back. I wondered if he would come back at all if it weren't for me.

The phone rang. I didn't have one in my room, of course, but there was one in the second-floor hallway.

"Hi, Annie," said Linda. "How's it going?"

"Not so great," I said. "Uncle Marco just left."

"Oh, that's too bad," she said perfunctorily. Her voice dropped. "Listen, Annie, you gotta help me out. Can you tell Jeff to meet me at Domino's at eight tonight? It's really important. Thanks a lot. I gotta run."

Dutifully, I called Jeff. Because of their parents, they didn't dare call each other and arrange their dates themselves.

"Oh, hi, Annie," Jeff said. "How's it going?"

"Not so great. Uncle Marco just left."

"Oh, I'm sorry to hear it." His voice dropped. "Uh, you hear anything from Linda?"

"She wants you to meet her at Domino's tonight at eight."

"Oh, great. Thanks a lot, Annie. See you on Monday."

I walked into my room and closed the door and thought about the boxes.

They were all I had of Uncle Marco. His room was as empty of personality as a hotel room. All his personal possessions, the things from his childhood, had been removed. Some he had taken away with him. Others Aunt Ruth had sold. He never used them, she said, and they were making clutter. When she got rid of them, she could rent the room out and make some money from it, since he was so rarely there. But she never rented it. Even though she could have made me do most of the work, a tenant still would have been a burden for her, and she was too lazy. And she really didn't need the extra money, despite what she said.

So the only mementos I had of Uncle Marco were the boxes.

I could hear the TV downstairs; Aunt Ruth was occupied. I opened the closet and squatted down and removed the old shoes and outgrown clothes I had piled on top of the gray metal box. I went over it carefully, stroking it. The surface was rough where it was stained and dented. There was no lip; it seemed to be permanently welded shut around the edges. But Uncle Marco had told me not to try to open it. That must mean there was a way to do it.

And that was when the overwhelming desire to open it came over me.

Of course, I felt guilty for even thinking of it. Uncle Marco was my favorite person in the world. How could I imagine doing something that he had so strongly told me not to do, something that would make him angry, that might even hurt him?

But Uncle Marco was a strange guy, always full of secrets. He never told me everything. He had told me absolutely nothing about the boxes, except not to open them. So what was their secret? And why had he left them with *me*, anyway? He must have had some other safer place, where they could be really locked up. They weren't very safe here, in a closet and in a basement, especially with nosy Aunt Ruth around. What could be his real reason be for leaving them here?

Could it be that he *wanted* me to open them?

No. That was ridiculous. I was just making excuses for my own curiosity—curiosity coming from my loneliness and from missing him. He had expressly told me not to even think of opening them, and he was serious when he said it.

And as I was telling myself this, my hands were running over the surfaces of the box, feeling for cracks or latches or keyholes. And finding nothing.

But the box in the basement was just a wooden crate. It might be easier to find some kind of opening on it. Anyway, even if I found something like that, it didn't mean I had to open it. I *wouldn't* open it, I told myself, pushing the metal box into the back of the closet and piling stuff up on it again. I would just go down to the basement and check out the wooden one.

CHAPTER FOUR

I went quietly down the stairs and crept across the front hallway so that Aunt Ruth, engrossed by the TV, wouldn't know I was going down to the basement.

Some basements have small half windows that let in a little daylight, but our basement was completely underground. There was a long, steep flight of wooden steps, and you had to feel your way down along the metal railing because there was no light switch at the top. Once you got to the bottom, you had to grope your way in the blackness, your hands above your head, until you found the chain that pulled on the bare ceiling bulb. It wouldn't have been very hard for Uncle Marco to make Aunt Ruth scared of coming down here.

The big old furnace in the main room was like a black monster with lots of tentacles, and right now it was hissing and rumbling softly with the effort to heat the house. There was an ancient washing machine with a hand-cranked wringer, which I had never seen anybody use; and trunks; and old cardboard boxes and piles of magazines from decades ago.

Beyond a cement wall with an open doorway was another, smaller room. You had to grope your way in there, too, reaching for the ceiling chain. Two of the walls in this room were made of stone, and there was a musty smell. Uncle Marco said it had once been a root cellar, where they stored vegetables in the days before refrigeration. Now there was nothing in here but more cardboard boxes and rusty tools on a wall covered with spiderwebs—and the wooden crate we had brought down here two days before.

I moved the cardboard boxes away from it and squatted down to study it in the dim light.

There were no visible nails. And at first, there didn't seem to be any differences between any of the surfaces. But as I looked at it more carefully, I noticed that the bottom of the box had a slight lip around it, as though it might be a lid. That meant I had to turn it over to see if it really was a lid or not.

I struggled with effort, grunting—it really was heavy. But

finally, bracing the crate with one foot, I managed to get it up on end. It was then, when it was balanced precariously, that I realized it would make too much noise if I just let it fall over on the cement floor; Aunt Ruth would hear it for sure. I was sweating now, as I held it there with one hand and one foot. I scrabbled with the other hand for the cardboard boxes I had piled around it earlier. They were just barely within my reach. I got a couple of them underneath it and let the box fall.

It made a dull thud, but not the crash it would have made otherwise. I waited, out of breath; there was no sign of life from Aunt Ruth. Thinking ahead now, I prepared a bed of cardboard boxes and old magazines and managed to tip the box over again. This time it hardly made a sound. Now the side with the lip was on top.

It did seem as though it might be a lid, but it was fixed immovably in place. I walked over to the wall behind me, the one with the tools on it.

There was a hammer and a chisel and a saw, and a small box of nails on the floor. I brought them all over. Then I just sat there again for a while, my heart pounding. Was I really, seriously going to try to do this? This thing that wonderful Uncle Marco had told me so strongly not to even *think* about doing? Uncle Marco, the only person in the world who I believed really loved me.

But why had he left the boxes with me, then? He said it was to keep them safe, but there had to be someplace safer than *here*. He was playing a game with me—he *wanted* me to open the box. You don't give somebody a box if you don't want her to open it.

Part of me knew I was lying to myself and that I should go upstairs right now and never come down here again. But life was just too depressing at this moment for me to resist such a mystery. What wonderful, exotic thing might be inside the box? I picked up the hammer and chisel and a piece of cardboard.

At first, the box didn't seem to want to be opened. And having to be quiet about it made the job a lot harder. I tapped away with the hammer and chisel, holding the piece of cardboard between them to dull the noise. I wasn't making any progress—until, at one corner, the chisel suddenly went in deeper, as though it had broken through a layer of tough adhesive. Encouraged, I worked around toward the back, chipping away. By the time I had done three sides, over an hour had gone by. Any minute, Aunt Ruth might yell for me. I was hoping the top was hinged so that now I could just lift it, instead of having to do two more corners and the last side.

I put down the hammer and chisel and began to lift. The lid was heavy—the inside seemed to be lined with metal —but the box opened a crack.

Something small and dark and crablike poked itself out of the crack. It turned briefly from side to side. Then it dropped to the floor with a hollow crackle and scuttled silently and much too fast across the room, zigzagging off into the darkness away from the doorway.

I dropped the lid, barely managing not to scream. There was something horrible about the way it had scrabbled sideways, speedy and determined yet not going in a straight line.

I held the lid down, terrified. The thing had seemed to be alive. But how could it stay alive, locked up in a box like this with no air vents? What kind of creature was it if it could live without air? And how many more were there inside? I was trembling now.

If there *were* others inside, at least they didn't seem to be trying to get out. The box was silent; nothing was pushing up against the lid.

I got up and forced myself to look around for the creature, even though I dreaded seeing it again and certainly couldn't imagine touching it—though I knew what I should really do was put it back inside the box. It hadn't gone past me through the doorway to the main basement room; it was still somewhere in the old root cellar. Feeling sick, I made myself pick up boxes and look under them, not knowing what I would do when I found it. It had to be in here somewhere.

The room was mostly empty. And yet I couldn't find the thing. It had vanished as suddenly as it had appeared. It must be waiting in some corner, hidden by its dark color. Waiting for what?

I tried to be logical, not hysterical. The thing was scary and ugly and inexplicable, but what could it really do? It was barely an inch long, and there was only one of it. If I couldn't find it, the most important thing to do was to prevent any others from getting out. I went back to the box, set a nail in place, and lifted the hammer.

But you can't hammer a nail quietly. Aunt Ruth would hear as soon as I struck the first blow. She might not come down to the basement, but she'd sure want to know what was going on. And how could I explain why I was hammering down here? I would have to wait until she went out, which might not be until she went to work on Monday. That was two days from now. In the meantime, I had to keep anything else from getting out of the box.

I went to the other room and got piles of magazines and set them on top of the box. I put the hammer and the box of nails and all the other tools on top of the magazines—a lot of the tools were metal, and all together they had to be really heavy. No more little creatures could get out of there. I piled more cardboard boxes all around it just in case Aunt Ruth *did* come down.

I snuck back upstairs. Aunt Ruth was still puffing away in front of the TV, not paying attention to anything else. I got back up to my room without being noticed.

I had expected the box to contain something beautiful and strange from some exotic corner of the world. Instead, all I had found was that almost mechanical crablike creature. Was it alive or what? What was it going to do?

My excuse for opening the box was that I had been depressed, but now I felt even worse, if possible. I had done what Uncle Marco had specifically asked me not to do, and when he came back he would know. I had never disobeyed him before; I had no idea how he would react. Now, instead of having something to look forward to, I was afraid.

Not to mention, I had let that horrible little thing escape from the box.

I tried to reassure myself. Maybe there had been some kind of fabric inside the box, an ethnic Bedouin wedding dress or something. And maybe the thing that came out was just some sort of harmless beetle that was eating the cloth, like moths ate wool. Maybe nothing else was going to happen. Maybe I should open the box all the way and see what was really inside it.

But if it was harmless, why had Uncle Marco told me not to open it? I was getting tired of thinking about it but was also too preoccupied to think about anything else. And I couldn't distract myself by calling my friends; I knew Linda and Jeff would be too excited about their date to pay much attention to what they would think was my stupid little problem. I knew I wouldn't be able to concentrate on studying or a book.

And so, to serve me right for the blunder I had made, I went down and watched TV with Aunt Ruth.

That night I had a very vivid dream. Uncle Marco was telling me to open the other box, the one in my closet. It was urgent; I had to do it without fail.

And he wasn't just telling me to open it. He was also telling me exactly how to do it.

CHAPTER FIVE

The dream didn't fade, as most dreams do. It was just as vivid when I woke up on Sunday morning. I remembered exactly how to open the metal box and how urgently Uncle Marco had been telling me to do it.

But I wasn't naive enough to believe that dreams were real messages. Everybody knew they were just psychological, your unconscious let loose or something. And it only made sense that my unconscious would be preoccupied with the boxes. I should just dismiss the dream and not pay any more attention to it.

Anyway, even as a message it didn't make sense. I knew Uncle Marco didn't want me to open the boxes—that's what he had told me, and I had never known him to lie. It was bad enough that I had already opened one of them; opening the other one, too, would only make it worse.

But what if the instructions in the dream worked? What would that mean? That it was not just something psychological, but a real message? Was it possible that, having opened one box, I could correct the damage only by opening the other one, too?

The phone rang. I hurried out to the hallway to answer it—Aunt Ruth didn't like to be awakened early on the weekends. It was Jeff. Maybe he could help me decide what to do about the boxes. As we started talking, I brought the phone into my room so Aunt Ruth wouldn't hear; the cord was just long enough for me to get it inside and close the door and stand there, but not long enough to get it over to the bed or the desk.

"Did you talk to Linda yet? What did she say about last night?" Jeff asked me, sounding worried.

"No, I didn't talk to her. What happened? Is something wrong?"

"Oh, we had a stupid fight. She was still mad when we said good-bye. I hate that! I need to find out if she forgave me yet. Tell her I'm sorry and to just forget the whole thing. I don't like having her mad at me. I'm worried."

"Okay, Jeff, I'll call her as soon as we get off the phone."

"Oh, that's great, Annie! What would we ever do without you? Call me back as soon as—"

"There was something I wanted to ask you about, too," I interrupted him.

"Yeah?" He sounded impatient.

"It has to do with these boxes Uncle Marco gave me. He told me I must never, never open—"

"That sounds really cool, Annie. I want to hear all about it. But I'm so worried about Linda I just can't concentrate on anything else right now. I know you understand. Can you call me as soon as you talk to her?"

I sighed. Of course, they were probably sick of hearing about Uncle Marco, I talked about him so much. If they had ever met him and seen what he was like, they would probably have been more interested, but for some reason he avoided meeting people as much as possible.

I called Linda. I asked her what their fight was about. She had been mad because Jeff hadn't noticed the new outfit she'd bought yesterday. Now she felt bad about it and wanted me to apologize. So I called Jeff back and told him. He was really relieved—but now something had come up and he didn't have time to talk with me about the boxes. I almost felt like getting angry, but I didn't. After all, they were my best friends. If I didn't help them, who would? And who else would I have to talk to? They might listen to me about the boxes tomorrow—if they weren't too busy whispering and giggling together.

I brought the phone out into the hall and then went back

to my room and closed the door. I took all the stuff off the box in the closet and squatted down beside it—I didn't want to pull it out in case Aunt Ruth came in.

I had decided what to do. If the instructions in the dream worked, then that meant it had to be a message, and I should follow it. If they didn't work, then it was just a meaningless dream. I wouldn't be able to open the box, and I'd be no worse off than I was already.

What I didn't think about at the time was, if the dream was a message, then who—or what—was it really from?

I put one hand on either side of the box. I moved them in circles in opposite directions, the right hand clockwise, the left hand counterclockwise—it was harder to do than you would think. After exactly thirty-nine rotations, I bent over and rested my forehead against the top of the box, continuing to move my hands. The box began to feel warm. After exactly eleven more rotations, I suddenly slapped the sides with my hands, bumped it lightly with my forehead, and sat back.

Nothing happened. The dream had not been a message after all. In a way, I was more relieved than disappointed.

And then, as I watched, the top of the box began to disintegrate, as if it were a piece of paper and an invisible fire was eating away at it from the center. In a moment it was gone. The box had no top anymore. There was no way to close it now.

Inside, almost filling it, was what looked more than anything else like a kind of propeller. It had four oddly shaped, curving blades, one pointing directly at each corner of the box. The blades were a couple of inches below the top of the box. In the center of the blades was a kind of dial, like a round combination lock. But instead of numbers, around the dial were funny-looking symbols, sort of like hieroglyphics.

Things that looked like thorns or roots, gnarled and twisting and branching, clung to the inside surfaces of the metal box.

I didn't like it; I didn't like it at all. I especially didn't like it that I couldn't close it. I started to back away from it.

And then there was a little click, and the dial in the center moved one tiny notch.

I jumped. The thing was doing something. By opening it, I must have activated it. Why had I ever done it? I thought of the horrible scrabbling thing I had released in the basement. How could I make the same stupid mistake twice in two days?

Maybe I could cover it with something, and that might stop it. I looked around inside the closet. On a shelf I found an old Scrabble game I used to play with Uncle Marco. When I unfolded the board, it was just a little bigger than the top of the box. I set it carefully in place. Now that the box was covered again, maybe it would stop. I got out of the closet and firmly closed the door.

I spent as much as possible of that Sunday away from my room. The basement was easy to avoid, but my room was another story. I brought my books and notebooks downstairs and did my homework at the dining room table. "Why aren't you studying upstairs?" Aunt Ruth wanted to know from in front of the TV in the living room. "It makes it hard for me to concentrate, with you over there shuffling papers."

Of course, I didn't tell her how hard the TV made it for me to concentrate. "I just felt like being around other people, that's all," I said. "I'm almost through with my homework. Then I can watch TV with you."

"I've never seen you so interested in TV before," Aunt Ruth said suspiciously. "Something funny about it." But then the TV drew her attention away from me.

When the phone rang, I automatically answered it; I knew who Aunt Ruth would and wouldn't talk to. "May I speak to Ruth Levi, please?" said a cool female voice.

"May I ask who's calling, please?"

"I'm calling on behalf of Crutchley Development, and it's urgent."

"She's not home," I said, feeling cold.

"Oh, isn't she?" the woman said, and even over the phone I could hear the sarcasm in her voice. "Well, sweetie, when she *does* come back, please tell her to call us—she knows the number. Everyone else in your neighborhood is signing purchase and sale agreements next week, and we need you and the Vails to sign, too. We'd appreciate it if she'd call right away—for her sake and yours." She hung up.

"Who was that?" Aunt Ruth wanted to know.

"That woman from Crutchley."

"Those pests are calling on *Sunday* now?" she said irritably.

"And . . . she was threatening," I told her. "She said everybody else is signing purchase and sale agreements next week, and she wants you to sign, too, and to call them as soon as possible—for your sake and mine."

Aunt Ruth blinked at me, pulling at her lower lip.

"And Henry told me the other night somebody was following him in a car when he was walking their dog. He was sure it was Crutchley—threatening him."

Aunt Ruth snorted. "Well, if they think they can badger me into giving in, they don't know who they're dealing with," she said and turned back to the TV.

Of course it never occurred to Aunt Ruth to worry that next time they might be following *me*.

I dreamed about Uncle Marco again that night. This time he was urging me to go down into the basement. But now I didn't believe the dream. I didn't think it was really Uncle Marco who was trying to give me this message.

And every couple of hours, it seemed, I would be awakened by a faint click from the closet. It seemed too quiet to be able to wake me up, and yet it did.

I had to open the closet on Monday morning to get something to wear to school. When I did, I saw that the Scrabble board had fallen off the box onto the floor. As though it had been pushed away.

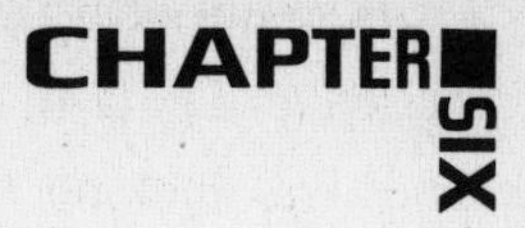

CHAPTER SIX

I was groggy and headachy in school that day because of having slept so badly. I was also very worried about what I had started by opening the boxes. I wanted to talk to Linda and Jeff about it—especially Jeff, because he was the practical one. But I also felt shy about mentioning it. Here in the everyday world of school the boxes seemed unreal, imaginary, dreamlike. How could I get anybody else to understand what was so scary about them?

I was also getting really worried about Crutchley Development. Why was everything going wrong all at once?

I was so out of it that I almost got caught passing a note from Jeff to Linda in math. Just in time I noticed that the teacher was looking in my direction, so I waited—which gave me a chance to read the note. It was just one of their typical boring notes. I passed it on when the coast was clear.

I didn't get a chance to talk to Linda and Jeff until lunch. Henry ate with us again today, too.

"You look tired today, Annie. Is something wrong?" Henry asked me as he sat down with us, sounding as if he actually cared.

Linda and Jeff were whispering together. They hadn't noticed that I looked tired. So why did I want to tell them about the boxes, rather than Henry? I guess I didn't feel I knew Henry well enough. He might think I was crazy.

But Henry and I did share a common problem: the situation with Crutchley. I told him about the phone call and how they wanted everybody to sign purchase and sale agreements this week. "Aunt Ruth said she wouldn't give in, no matter what," I finished.

Henry frowned. "Well, I guess that's good. I just hope they don't start following you. I'd be really worried if that happened. So you're tired because you were worried about Crutchley and didn't sleep well?" he asked me.

"I didn't sleep well, but not because of worrying about Crutchley," I told Henry. "Bad dreams."

"What kind of bad dreams?"

I looked around. Linda and Jeff still weren't paying any

attention. Weren't they even curious? All I ever did was help them, and they wouldn't even listen to me. It dawned on me then how totally one-sided our relationship was, and that made me angry. Why should I share my confidences with *them*?

I turned back to Henry. "It was kind of more *vivid* than any other dream I ever had," I told him.

Henry leaned forward. He was blond and lanky and had big blue eyes. "Yeah? Go on."

"I dreamed somebody important to me gave me two boxes to keep safe for him and told me I must never open them; I mustn't even *think* about opening them. And then the person who gave them to me left." I paused. "If that happened to you, what would *you* do?"

He shrugged. "I'd keep them safe, like he told me."

"You wouldn't try to open them?"

"Of course not. He told you not to, right?" Henry said it with total conviction. "So what else happened in your dream?"

His attitude made me too embarrassed to admit I had even dreamed about opening the boxes, let alone that I had actually done it in real life. "Well, that was it, I guess," I said, my voice a little shaky. "I wanted to open them and I had to keep fighting the temptation. I almost gave in—and that was when I woke up."

"Hmmmm," he said thoughtfully. "There's probably some deep psychological meaning to it, but I'm not good at that stuff." Then he looked worried. "But I still don't understand why it bothers you so much, Annie. I mean, it was just a dream—and not even that scary. It would have been different if you'd opened them."

"Yeah," I mumbled.

He smiled. "I'm going to have to start calling you Pandora."

"Pandora? Who's Pandora?"

"It's a Greek legend." Henry was smart; I had to admit that—there was more to him than I had realized. "It happened when the world was still perfect. Nobody had any problems. There was no war. Nobody was sick. Nobody died. Then somebody—some god in disguise or something—gave a box to a girl named Pandora and told her to keep it safe for him and to never open it. But she was too curious. She opened it."

"Yeah?" I could hardly believe how similar this story was to mine. "And then what happened?"

"All these terrible, hideous, ugly creatures came swarming out." Henry flailed his arms. "They were all the problems of the world. Before that, the world had been a perfect place. Then Pandora let all the bad things out—disease, war, death, everything. Now the world was real life—full of horrible problems."

"And that's the end?" I said, horrified.

"No. One last thing came out of the box—beautiful, not ugly. Her name was Hope. And now hope is the only thing we have going for us."

I was so upset by the story I didn't know what to say. Luckily, the bell rang.

For the rest of the day I kept worrying about what Henry had said. I knew this Pandora thing was just a story, but even so, it made what I had done seem more terrible, more dangerous.

I took my time going home. And after I got home, I kept thinking of things to do away from my closet. Finally, after more than an hour, I worked up the nerve to look inside.

At first glance, the box seemed pretty much the same. Then I noticed, with a cold feeling, that the propeller blades had moved slightly. They were no longer pointing exactly into the corners of the box, but about a quarter of an inch off. It also seemed that the propeller was slightly higher than it had been, now maybe an inch and a half below the top edge of the box. Was it slowly turning, moving upward? I didn't even want to think about it.

But I couldn't help noticing that the rootlike things clinging to the inside of the box were branching out a little; the ends of them almost looked like veiny hands.

There was a faint click, and the dial in the center moved one notch. I shivered and carefully put the Scrabble board on top of it again.

And what was happening in the basement?

I knew I had to check it out. If something weird was going on down there, I needed to know about it. I tried to tell myself that the thing that had run out of the box was probably just some sort of mothlike creature that had been eating the Bedouin wedding dress or whatever was inside the box. It wasn't so easy to believe this now, though, after seeing what was inside the box in my closet.

I had to go down right away, before Aunt Ruth came home and got suspicious.

I went very slowly, listening in the darkness on the stairs. I didn't know what I expected to hear, but all I did hear was the faint rumbling hum of the furnace.

And then, as I neared the bottom of the stairs, I began to feel it. An intrusion in my head, a tingling, working from outside to deeper inside. Was I truly going crazy now?

The tingling grew stronger as I stepped down onto the basement floor; my brain felt almost like it was glowing. And for the first time in my life I didn't have to grope around for the chain to turn on the light: I just reached up with my hand and there it was, in exactly the right place. I hesitated, unable to imagine what the light would show me. Then I clenched my teeth and pulled the chain.

There was nothing unusual in the main room except for the peculiar electric sensation in my head. But the box—and the creature—had been in the root cellar. I went that way. My head seemed to be pulling me there. I stepped into the small, dark room. I reached up without thinking and there was the chain for the light—again, no groping. I pulled it.

The room looked exactly the same. There was the wooden box, with cardboard boxes piled around it and magazines and tools holding down the lid. I could see no sign of the little creature.

But the inside of my head was full of sensation. Not words, exactly, but meaning, thoughts, pushing in from outside.

Greetings. Welcome. I am happy you finally showed up. Have you eaten yet?

I put my hands to my ears. "Huh? *Eaten* yet? Who is this? What's going on?" I said, dazed, feeling crazier than ever.

I do not understand your language. Please communicate directly, as we do.

The terrified part of me wanted to run away. But the curious part of me was fascinated, rooted to the spot. The sensations in my head weren't threatening. And the little creature—if that's where the thoughts were coming from—seemed shy, keeping hidden from me, not attacking. It couldn't understand me talking, only thinking. *Why do you want to know if I've eaten yet?* I mentally asked it.

A polite greeting, that is all. Nothing here for you to eat anyway.

That was when I noticed a neat conical pile of what looked like iron filings, which hadn't been there before, in one corner of the room. I moved toward it. On closer inspection, I could see that it was more like gray sand. *What's this?* I thought, moving my foot toward it.

Please. Do not touch with foot. Very bad manners. Even

though that is only waste product. The walls of this room are not very tasty yet, but soon we—

You're going to eat the walls?

Not polite to interrupt. I was saying, the walls of this room are not very tasty yet, but soon we will have the right seasoning and spices to make them very delicious.

Soon they would have the right seasoning and spices? I didn't like the sound of that. I especially didn't like the way it kept saying *we. How many of you are there, anyway?*

Two, in just a moment.

Now I was poking around, actively looking for the creature. It seemed to me that the mental sensations were coming from somewhere near the wooden box. I was very scared, of course. But it still hadn't done or said anything threatening, and I couldn't control my curiosity—the same way I hadn't been able to control my curiosity about the boxes. I pushed aside Henry's story about Pandora and how she had released all the problems of the world because of her curiosity. I moved one of the cardboard boxes aside, then another.

And then I saw it and screamed.

CHAPTER SEVEN

What was horrible was how much it had grown. The last time, it had been the size of one of those tiny sand crabs that make holes in the beach, no bigger than a beetle. Now it was the size of a guinea pig or a gerbil. And it wasn't running away—I could see what it really looked like. I felt sick. And yet, even though I wanted to run from it, I couldn't.

It had a disk-like body and six legs. Actually, only the back four limbs seemed to be legs, planted firmly on the floor. It was rubbing the front two together, like a fly. I couldn't see much of a face, only a ridged triangular head.

The mouth seemed to be closed, and the other features, if there were any, were buried in the ridges.

Beside it lay a soft-looking, round grayish object, like an opaque soap bubble. As I watched, tiny teeth tore away at the bubble from the inside. In a moment, another creature had emerged from the gray shreds, identical to the small one that had rushed out of the box the other day.

Welcome, baby.

The small one put its arms on the floor and deeply bowed its head to the large one, apparently a gesture of respect. *Honor to my parent,* piped a little voice in my head. Then the smaller one scampered off, dashing around the room in the same odd, zigzag way its parent had moved when I first let it out of the box.

Wait a minute. I thought you said there was only one of you before you had the baby. How can only one single creature produce an offspring?

The meaning you have is . . . parthenogenesis. You must have some reference work that will explain. We need only one individual to reproduce.

So, what that means is, it didn't stop anything that I only let one of you out of the box. You can still have babies and babies.

One individual is all that is necessary to reproduce. And now that you can see me, I greet you. It put its arms to the floor and bowed its head in the same way the baby had done to it. *I do not sense you return the greeting,* it said, with a testy tone.

I held my arms in front of me and bowed my head. *Like that?*

Close enough, from what I can sense. We do not perceive waves of light. In your way of thinking we are blind. And of course that will be your job. If you pass. That is why we may allow you to be a part of the three-in-one. That is why we asked you to activate the supreme being, the Lord—the Lord we can never "see."

Everything it said was strange, but now it was getting stranger by the second—and more ominous. How soon would the basement be full of them, once they both started producing more babies? How would I keep them hidden from Aunt Ruth? And was it this creature that had sent me the dream to open the box upstairs? Was that what it meant by "activate the supreme being"?

I didn't like the sound of any of it. But I was too curious to just ignore it!

Of course you will not ignore us! We think you should appreciate the great honor we may bestow upon you. Appreciate—and be ready to begin your functioning. Your first sensate function is your test—to study the face of the Lord with your sense organs that perceive waves of light and to ask it for a slowdown. Then you will return and convey to us—

Wait a minute. I don't know if I understand what you're talking about. And I don't know if I agreed to anything yet.

I am incapable of hiding from you my feeling that foreigners like you are very slow-witted. You will understand all very soon, I hope—otherwise we will have to find another. And why do I not detect your sense of joy and honor at possibly being part of the three-in-one?

What is *the three-in-one? Why is it an honor to be part of it?*

You will understand if you pass. Now go and look at the face of the Lord. Give it this offering. Ask it very politely for a slowdown. Come back and communicate to us what it says.

What it says? You mean it talks?

It is one heck of an effort to maintain my patience with you! Give this to it, and make gesture of respect, and ask for slowdown, and come back and tell me what you see. Time for you to go now.

Its hands moved too fast for me to see exactly how it happened, but in the next moment a small scrap of something shiny and metallic lay on the floor in front of it. It bowed to the scrap of metal three times. *Now present this gift to the Lord and tell us what you see. Now!*

I bent over and picked up the little scrap of metal. It felt like a piece of foil. I left the lights on and pounded up the stairs fast. It was after five; Aunt Ruth would be home soon.

I approached the box in my room. The Scrabble board had been pushed away again—it obviously didn't want to be covered.

The creatures in the basement, the ones who came out of the wooden box—they wanted me to give you this, I thought at it. *And they ask you very politely for a slowdown.*

Could it really understand? Except for the rootlike hands, which might be plants, the rest of it seemed to be a machine. *They call you the Lord. They respect you a lot. This is a gift for you. They ask you to make a slowdown. They want to know what you say to them.*

I set the piece of foil in the center, near the dial. And, feeling foolish, I bowed my head to it in the gesture of respect.

There must have been a small gust of wind. I don't know where it came from, since all the windows were closed. But the little scrap of foil fluttered off the propeller and over to one of the branching tendrils.

Slowly, with a faint creaking sound, the root closed around it. My stomach felt cold.

And then the dial moved, faster than I'd ever seen it. Not one notch, like before, but several notches. It was now pointing at a symbol that looked like a sideways letter eight. Then it stopped.

Was this the message the thing downstairs wanted me to convey? I didn't have time to wonder. I looked at my watch. It was 5:25. Aunt Ruth would be home at any minute.

I dashed down to the basement and into the root cellar. The creatures were waiting there. Astonishingly, the smaller one had grown already and was almost the same size as the larger one; the pile of crumbled rock in the corner was bigger.

It accepted the gift. One of the things like hands took it. And then it moved the dial in the middle over to this.

I projected a strong mental picture of the sideways number eight.

The two creatures didn't look at each other—after all, they couldn't see. But they did a funny little jig, jumping around in circles. I wondered what senses they used to navigate around if they didn't have eyesight. Maybe they had some kind of sonar, like bats. That could be why they always moved in a zigzag pattern, bouncing sound waves off the walls.

Then they both bowed to me. I was learning; now I bowed back without being told.

A good sign, they both thought at me. *Now we can proceed. And now we know you understand. You will be allowed to be the nervous system of the three-in-one.*

The nervous system? I was baffled.

Then it hit me. Odd, how something so peculiar could feel so familiar. *I think I understand now. I'm . . . I'm the messenger.*

You just passed the test.

Upstairs the front door slammed. "Anne, come down this minute!" Aunt Ruth bellowed. "I need some help. You have to make some phone calls to people I don't want to talk to."

There was no way to hide that I had been in the basement. I would have to say I felt cold and was checking on the furnace or something. I hurried upstairs, wondering if she would believe me. Well, even if she didn't, and even if she overcame her fear of the basement to check on it herself, the creatures would probably know enough to hide. Aunt Ruth wouldn't notice anything was different. Nothing much had physically changed in the basement, after all.

But when I went down there the next day after school, that was no longer true.

CHAPTER EIGHT

"You don't look much better today, Annie," Henry said at lunch the next day. He was paying more attention to me than ever these days. Was he attracted to the dark circles under my eyes, or what?

"Oh, I'm still having sleeping problems, I guess," I said. Actually, it was nice that someone was genuinely interested in me as a person and not just in my ability to give messages. And even though I knew there was no way I could ever tell Henry what was really going on, it was a relief to have somebody to confide in, at least a little bit.

It was also a relief that he didn't tell me I was talking too fast, as everybody else had done today, starting with Aunt Ruth.

"Was it that dream again?" Henry asked me, and I couldn't help being pleased that he remembered.

Linda and Jeff, as usual, weren't paying any attention. But today there was something oddly sluggish and drawn out about their whispering and giggling. Their voices seemed a little deeper. What was the matter with them? The entire cafeteria, in fact, was hushed and subdued.

"Yes, that dream again," I said, and now I dared to admit, "except this time, I *did* open the boxes. Just like that girl, Pan . . . Pan . . ."

"Pandora," Henry said, looking worried now. "Maybe it's my fault for telling you that story. So what happened? Did all the problems in the world come out?"

"No. Not all the problems in the world. But it was pretty weird."

"Yeah?" he said, leaning forward. "What happened?"

"Oh, it's too boring," I said. "Nobody's really interested in other people's dreams."

"I am," he insisted. "At least your dreams, anyway."

So I told him—about the creatures in the basement and the weird propeller-clock thing upstairs. I knew it was supposed to be a secret; Uncle Marco had told me not to tell anybody about the boxes. But Henry believed it was just a dream, so what harm could that do? Anyway, I had already done something much worse: I had opened the boxes. And I needed somebody to talk to about this, even though Henry believed it was only a dream. It was too scary to deal with alone.

I told him in pretty much detail. I kept thinking the bell would ring, but it didn't.

When I finished, he sat back on the orange plastic cafeteria chair, scratching his head. "Gee, I wish I had dreams like that," he said. "Mine are always so vague and meaningless. This one is like . . . a story."

"Yeah, but not a very nice story," I said unhappily.

"Well, those little bugs in the basement are kind of creepy," he admitted. "But that propeller–clock thing, that's cool. I wonder if it has something to do with time, like if it manages time somehow."

"What do you mean by *that*?"

The bell gradually rang.

Henry looked at his watch. "Funny," he said. "Lunch seemed to last so long today." He looked worried. "But don't get me wrong," he hastily added. "It wasn't because I was bored or anything. I'd like to talk more about your dream." He thought for a moment. "Math seemed to last a long time, too, but that's normal. See you in band."

Everything *had* seemed to go on longer than usual today, I now realized. It made my head feel funny. The other kids were dragging out of the cafeteria, getting in my way. Was I catching the flu, or what?

Band practice was after school. Henry played the tuba

and I played the piccolo, so we didn't sit near each other. We were working on a very corny Sousa march that everybody had heard a million times before. Only today, Mr. Lang, who normally tried to get us to play faster, was taking all the tempos very, very slow. The band sounded like a tape being played at the wrong speed. I almost asked the flute player next to me what was going on. But nobody else acted like anything was unusual, so I didn't say anything.

I looked over at Henry. He seemed to be having a terrible time getting any sound out of the tuba, his cheeks red and puffed, sweat on his forehead. I was having trouble making the piccolo do anything right myself. Band practice droned on forever and ever. The music had never sounded so stodgy.

Henry walked me home afterward. "Feel my forehead, Annie. I think I might be coming down with something."

I pulled off my gloves. "It feels normal to me," I said, comparing his temperature to mine. "I thought I felt sick today, too. What's the matter?"

"I could hardly play my tuba at all. It took too much effort."

"I felt the same way. And didn't all the tempos seem really draggy?"

He turned to me. "Yes! Was Mr. Lang asleep or what?" He thought for a moment. "Maybe we're *both* coming down with something." Then he turned and glanced over his shoulder. His voice dropped. "Don't look, but there's that car again—the one that was following me the other night."

I looked; I couldn't help it. It was a long, dark car, and it was creeping along very slowly behind us. The windows were tinted; I couldn't see the driver.

"Wow, I'm glad you're with me," I blurted out without thinking.

Henry smiled. "I am, too," he said.

"Where's . . . the . . . fire . . . you . . . two?" an old lady croaked deeply at us, smiling, as we passed a bus stop.

"No fire," I told her, puzzled. She stared after us for a long, long time.

All the cars were going quite slowly, but the one behind us was the slowest, keeping at our pace.

It followed us through the crumbling stone gate that was the entrance to our neighborhood. The neighborhood was only four blocks, but it was the oldest area in the suburb, with Victorian brick and stone buildings and larger yards and lots of big old trees. Most of the houses were in disrepair; people couldn't afford all the upkeep they needed. No one in the city seemed to be interested in buying and fixing up houses like this, which was why Crutchley was in a good position to get people to sell.

The car stopped just beyond my house as we walked up to the porch.

"You can come in and wait until the car goes away," I said. "Except you'll have to leave before Aunt Ruth comes home." I checked my watch. I was home late because of band. "Four-twenty," I said. "She always gets home at five-thirty."

"I wish I could, but I have to hurry home," he said. "My mother's going out and I'm fixing dinner."

"What if that car follows you?"

"What can happen in the middle of the day?" he said, making an effort to sound bright. "I'll hurry—he's going really slow." He shook his head, perplexed. "So weird! Everything's so slow today except you and me. Are we going crazy?"

"I don't feel crazy, except for that," I said.

"Oh, well. Maybe we'll feel better tomorrow. See you."

In my closet, the clock dial was clicking away at more frequent intervals now. The propellers had moved farther; they were now pointing at the middle of the sides of the box. And they were higher, too, only about half an inch below the top.

The tendrils had crawled up to the top. One of them was clutching at the edge.

Was it because of the message and the gift I had given it yesterday that it was moving more quickly? But I had asked it for a slowdown, whatever that was.

I remembered how Uncle Marco had told me to think carefully about where to put each box. Now I wished I had put the wooden one up here and the clock downstairs. My little "friends" in the basement seemed benign in comparison to the thing in my closet. I went down to check on how they were doing.

Of course, yesterday Aunt Ruth had asked me why I

would go to check on the furnace if I had no idea how it really worked. I said I just wanted to see if it was running. It was pretty lame, but she was eager for me to make some phone calls for her, so she let it pass. And she didn't go down to the basement. But I didn't want to get caught down there again. Even though there wasn't much to see, I didn't want Aunt Ruth anywhere near the box.

By this time I could go down the stairs quite quickly in the dark. I felt the warmth growing in my head as I descended. At the bottom, without even thinking about where the chain was, I just reached up and instantly pulled on the light. I strolled over to the root cellar, the glow inside my head increasing, and pulled on the light in there.

And then I squeezed my eyes shut, momentarily dazzled. Opening them again slowly, my heart thudding, I listened to the many voices singing in my head.

A tall structure now rose up around the box, a three-dimensional grid made from strands of some dark fiber that reflected bright flashes from the ceiling lightbulb. There were little ladders and platforms all over it, and dozens of creatures were scurrying up and down them. The structure shuddered precariously with their movement. It went all the way up to the ceiling and back to the wall.

How had they done all this so fast? How had they had so many offspring so quickly?

Greetings. Welcome.

I looked down to see a large one bowing to me from the

floor. I didn't know if it was the original one or not, but I was glad to see it still wasn't any bigger than a gerbil. None of them were; I hoped that meant that they were their full adult size and wouldn't get any bigger.

Greetings, I thought at it and bowed my head, too.

You did your job well yesterday, nervous system, it told me. *That is what has made all of this possible. Good thing, too! Now we are whole, three-in-one.*

This thing you built. What is it? It's . . . beautiful.

You speak very well. You are very intelligent, it flattered me. *Of course, we do not perceive our home as you do, through waves of light. But we can sense its future beauty also.*

But how did you do it so fast? How did you have enough time to build this and also have so many babies?

Foreigners! it complained, not so flattering now. *Can't you understand the way things work? You are the nervous system. We asked the Lord through you, and it granted our request to give us the slowdown.*

"Huh?" I said aloud. I didn't know what it was talking about. It was also not as easy to understand as before because there was so much more background noise now, like a kind of constant, fluctuating, high-pitched whistle. It must be the mental pitch of the sonar all the creatures were using to get around. It wasn't very loud, but it was distracting.

And then I sensed unusual movement and looked up

high. The creatures near the top were scrawnier than the ones lower down, I noticed, and their color was blotchy—they looked unhealthy. A very large number of these were all rushing up one small ladder at the same time, right at the top. The ladder was trembling, the entire structure swaying wildly, dangerously now. *Hey!* I thought. *Wait! Maybe you should—*

The ladder shuddered and then broke in two. All the creatures on it, and the broken ladder, plummeted to the ground, tearing the structure on the way down. When the creatures splatted on the floor, they lay still, the torn fibers above them swaying slowly.

There was a sound like an alarm in my head. The fallen creatures were quickly surrounded by others who, slowly for them, carried the bodies away someplace behind the box where I couldn't see them.

Very terrible, oh, very terrible! the large one near me was saying, and I was almost aware of emotion in its voice. *Very many workers gone! And now all we gained from the slowdown is lost. Why has the Lord done this to us?*

Yeah, but . . . the ladder wasn't strong enough for so many. They should have been more careful, taken precautions.

It ignored my advice. *We must dance! We must do special ceremony! You will watch and see everything in the waves of light. And then you will convey everything to the Lord. It makes the Lord very happy for us to dance to it.*

After that, it will help us more after our disaster. Come! It rubbed its little arms together. Others began to gather around it. They now had little pieces of the foil substance tucked into the ridges in their heads, like funny hats.

Wouldn't it be better to just make stronger ladders? I suggested.

Do not disturb us now. Watch, remember, and convey. You are the nervous system.

For about five minutes they pranced around in a circle, stopping often to bow deeply. At the end they all removed their little foil hats and put them in a pile on the floor. *Take these offerings to the Lord,* one of them instructed me. *Convey our ritual to it. Tell it about our disaster and ask it to help—to make deeper slowdown so we can repair our population and finish our home in time. We know it needs our home. But remind it gently. Be polite! Go! Hurry!*

It wasn't being polite. I didn't like the way it was ordering me around, and I wished it could at least say please.

And it picked up the thought, without me even trying to project it. *Okay, okay, we thank you very much,* came the sensation in my head. *Now you can go.*

I hurried upstairs.

In my closet I bowed to the clicking propeller. I placed the little pieces of foil in the center of it. I concentrated on the images of the disaster and the ritual in the basement. I thanked it very much and said they needed more help, a deeper "slowdown." I was beginning to think I understood what the word meant, impossible as it seemed. I stood there and waited to see what it would do with the pieces of foil.

Again, there was a gust of wind, even though no window was open. But this time the pieces of foil didn't fall into the tendrils. They were blown forcefully up into the air and landed outside the box on the closet floor. The offerings were rejected.

And then my vision blurred for an instant, and when it cleared, I saw four babies of the basement creatures, one on each blade of the propeller. My vision blurred again, and then the babies were gone. The message was clear.

The pieces of foil weren't enough anymore.

CHAPTER NINE

I went back downstairs slowly, shivering a little. I had been afraid of the clock from the first moment I saw it, and it just kept getting more sinister. Why did it want their offspring?

Creepy as they were, I almost felt sorry for the little creatures downstairs now. They worshiped this thing, they called it Lord, they gave it gifts. And look how it responded.

When I walked into the root cellar they were already standing there, stunned. The buzz of their brains and of their sonar had come almost to a complete stop. They had taken the information from my brain already.

Then the sonar buzz began again. They all turned and pointed their ridged heads up, toward the top level of the grid structure.

I put my hand to my mouth as a sudden fight broke out among the scrawny, blotchy ones at the top of the structure. The babies rose up on their back legs, scrabbling furiously at each other with their front ones, slashing with their jaws. The structure trembled; I was afraid more were going to fall off.

In a minute or two the fight was over. Slowly, the four losing babies from the highest level began climbing down. The accident had happened near the top, too; the ones who had died then were also the scrawnier, blotched ones.

They are of the lowest class, came a direct voice inside my head. *Naturally it is from the lowest class that victims come.*

I didn't project my thoughts directly, but it still knew what I was thinking. *Unfair? I do not understand why you are worrying about that. That is what the lower classes are for—sacrifice, obligation. Their lives aren't worth much. You can carry them now. They are ready to be taken to the Lord. They offer themselves.*

I realized then, belatedly, that in order to get them upstairs I was going to have to touch them. So far I had managed to avoid that. *Wait a minute. Do they really have to give up their lives? What if you just didn't do what the Lord asked?*

I was shaken by a silent howl of rage and horror at this

suggestion. The clock was all-powerful; it could not be disobeyed.

Gritting my teeth, I lifted my hands to where the four infants were waiting at the edge, at about the level of my shoulders. Moving their heads back and forth, two of them crawled onto my left, two onto my right hand. They weighed hardly anything; the touch of their legs was like the brush of a feather. I was relieved that they were not sticky or slimy. I moved with them toward the door.

And then I was struck by exactly what it was I was doing. I turned back. *I won't do this! I won't take them up there to that thing. I don't want to have anything to do with—*

Suddenly the creatures in my hands were painfully stinging me. Reflexively I tried to shake them off. They wouldn't fall off, glued to my hands.

What they are doing is involuntary; they don't want to go either. Their bodies are doing it because you are not fulfilling your function. The pain will stop when you get going.

I protested mentally, still shaking my hands. The pain got worse.

You are the nervous system. The combined voices of the whole group were very powerful.

I stamped my foot in outrage. The pain got even worse. Furious, I turned and started for the door again. The pain stopped instantly.

Halfway up from the basement the mental sensations

from the others faded, and I could distinguish the impulses from the ones I carried. They were terrified, and feeling it made me wonder what I could do. I began to climb more slowly.

The creatures weren't glued to my hands anymore. Each pair was pressing their heads together, their front legs extended in a clumsy embrace. They were trying to comfort each other! I felt the beginnings of tears behind my eyes.

I quickly knelt, my hands on the floor. *Run away! Now! Before—*

They were glued to my hands again, stinging me.

When I reached my room, I heard the click of the clock dial moving a notch. Was there a self-satisfied, gloating tone to it?

Like a robot, I walked into the closet. I deposited one of the little creatures on each propeller blade, my tears welling up now. I started to turn away.

But I couldn't. I had to watch. I was too curious not to.

They stood there on the propellers, fear radiating from them like waves of heat from a summer pavement. And the clock waited. It clicked, and clicked again. The propellers jerked a tiny bit. The four creatures were trembling now. And still nothing happened.

Was the clock enjoying this?

Then a tendril slowly detached from the side of the box and draped itself over the edge of the nearest propeller. Its movement so gradual that it was barely perceptible, it snaked toward the little waiting creature, which was shaking so violently now it could barely stand. Its fear was a wail inside my head. But it didn't back away. It stood firm when the root reached it. The tendrils separated, then wrapped themselves around it. And slowly, slowly squeezed. When I heard a cracking sound, I turned away. In my mind I felt the stab of broken carapace piercing the flesh.

It took a long time to die; the clock made sure of that. And so did the other three. Tears streamed down my face from the mental shadow of their pain. And I swore I would never do this again, no matter what.

I looked back at the clock as soon as the last one was gone. The propellers jerked, the dial clicked, and clicked again, and then again. The clock was speeding up, no doubt about that; it was going a lot faster now.

I stepped away from the closet, feeling sick. I turned to start downstairs. I glanced out the window as I went past. And then I spun back and stared.

The cars were moving even more slowly than they had been earlier this afternoon, when I was with Henry. And as I watched, it was as though they were all gradually putting on their brakes at exactly the same rate. Slower and slower, until you had to stare and look at them in relation to a tree to be sure they were moving at all. The pedestrians had become lifelike statues.

I was clenching my teeth, my hand pulling at my lip. How could this be happening? I hurried away from the window, then turned back and looked again. Finally I rushed out of the room and down the stairs.

A terrible thought was spinning around my brain. Was the clock doing this to time because of the offering I had carried out, as the nervous system—as the messenger? Was it my fault?

Like me, my friends in the basement weren't frozen. My brain fizzled with their patterns as they raced up and down their shaking, unstable grid, repairing the damage that had been done and adding new sections. Like spiders, they spun the construction material out of their own bodies. Was it digested rock?

Be careful! If you don't watch it, you'll have another accident!

We must hurry. We need more room. And the Lord wishes us to complete construction as soon as possible. That is why the Lord has graciously made such a powerful slowdown.

I didn't want to watch, afraid every instant that there would be another disaster. I turned off the light and hurried upstairs. As I reached the top, I glanced at my watch. It was 4:25. Only five minutes had gone by since I had last looked at it, outside the house with Henry, though it felt more like an hour to me. I had to stare at it for a very long time before the second hand moved.

I was panicking now. This was worse than any nightmare. Everything had almost stopped, except for me and the creatures. Would it ever start up again? Upstairs, I looked out the window. It was horrifying and disorienting, but addictive. I kept turning away, then looking back. I had never felt so helpless and alone.

But something was telling me that I wasn't really alone, that there was another individual who probably had not slowed down like the rest of the world.

Henry! Henry had not been part of the sickly sluggishness of everything at school today. If he had been outside of the slowdown then, he would probably be outside of it now, too.

I raced to the phone and opened the phone book. But the first handful of pages I flipped tore out in slow motion, then hung in midair, rocking lazily back and forth as they took their time descending toward the floor. What was happening? Why were the pages disintegrating?

They weren't disintegrating. It was just that I was moving so much faster than the rest of the world that I had accidentally ripped them. I had to be careful. As if handling an ancient manuscript, I very cautiously and delicately turned the pages until I found Henry's number.

I lifted the receiver. The dial tone was not a tone, but a series of clearly separated rumbles. Would the phone even work? Gingerly, I touched the first button of Henry's number, thinking about not pushing too fast or too hard. There was resistance at first. Then the button slowly, slowly sank down, as if into deep, dense mud. The vibrato tone of what was normally a beep lasted what seemed like five minutes.

It took forever to dial the number. And then I had to wait through the rings and the long silences between them, each one going on and on and on. It was like being put on hold, multiplied by a million. I was impatient to find out if Henry was experiencing all this. And I had to wait, wait, and wait in helpless frustration. Would he ever answer?

Then there was a clashing and rumbling, like a long, drawn-out roll of thunder. Ten minutes I waited through it, and finally there was a voice. "Hello?" Henry said, sounding very tentative.

"Henry, it's me, Annie."

"Annie . . ." He waited for a moment. Then *"Annie!"* he shouted joyously. "I should have known! Because you saw it in school today, when it was a lot less than this. I'm not going crazy? It's happening to you, too!"

I was too scared, and too excited that I was not alone, to think. "It's not just happening to me, Henry," I told him. "I think . . . I *did* it."

That was when it really hit me for sure: I *had* been part of what made this happen.

Henry hesitated. "Huh?"

"I gave the message that made the world stop. It's because of the boxes. And I'm their messenger."

"You mean that dream?" he said, confused and also skeptical.

"It's not a dream." Part of me knew I shouldn't be telling him this, but the main part of me was out of control. "It's real. I only said it was a dream. My uncle Marco, who's always going to strange, secret places, left the boxes here and told me not to open them. But I did open them, and then the whole world went crazy. I'm as bad as Pandora! It's all my fault."

"Are you sure you . . . know what you're saying, Annie?" Henry said carefully, as though he were talking to a crazy person.

"Come over and see for yourself. We have plenty of time. Oodles and oodles of time." I was on the verge of hysteria. "Aunt Ruth won't be home for days at this rate." I glanced at my watch. "Come over and see for—"

The second hand darted forward. And then, only a moment later, it shot forward again. It was quickly approaching 4:26.

"Okay, Annie, I'll be right—"

"Wait a minute," I said slowly. "Check it out, Henry. I think it's stopping. Or, I mean, the world is *starting* again."

Through the living room window I could see the cars uniformly inching forward, gradually accelerating.

"You're right," Henry breathed, awe in his voice. "And it's happening fast. But I still want to come over and see these boxes."

"No. There isn't time now. Aunt Ruth will be home in an hour," I said.

Time was racing back to normal; I was flooded with guilt. It was bad enough that I had opened the boxes. Now I had made it even worse by telling somebody about them.

For my whole life, I had always done whatever people

told me to do. Not until the last few days had I ever disobeyed anyone—Uncle Marco, my favorite person in the world. How was I ever going to undo what I had done?

"Henry," I said. "Just, uh . . . just forget I ever called you."

"You can't tell me something like that and expect me to forget it, Annie," Henry said. "I have to see those boxes soon. There's no way around it."

"Not now, Henry," I said. "Not now. See you tomorrow." I hung up.

Cars were speeding by normally outside; clocks ticked away. Aunt Ruth would be home in an hour, and I'd have to act like nothing had happened. I started upstairs to try to prepare myself.

I heard the front door open. I turned around on the stairs.

Aunt Ruth waddled inside, carrying bundles. She looked up at me. Then she frowned. "What's the matter with you?" she demanded. "You're staring at me like I'm a ghost or something."

I made an effort to sound calm, not panicky. I glanced at my watch. It was 4:30. "I just . . . didn't expect you home now."

"Were you up to something?" She glanced quickly around, as if searching for evidence against me.

"No. I just . . ." I didn't know what to say.

"Don't you remember anything? I told you I was taking off early today. I had to do some shopping. Probably a mistake—I bet the bank will be a mess when I go back in the morning. Can't do without me for one afternoon. Anyway, I came back here now because I want to talk to Crutchley —in private."

"Crutchley?" I said, remembering the car that had followed us. What had happened since then had blotted it out of my mind. "I think Crutchley was following me and—following me home today," I said. "The same way they were threatening Henry the other night. It was kind of scary. What do you want to talk to them about?"

She came inside and slammed the door, then turned back to me. "Don't just stand there! Can't you see how much I'm carrying?"

She wasn't going to tell me about Crutchley; she wasn't concerned about the threat to me. And she was behaving as though everything were normal. It was clear: She hadn't noticed what had happened this afternoon.

After I had helped Aunt Ruth, Linda called with a message for Jeff. After calling him, I closed myself in my room, thinking hard. As far as I could tell, everybody else was unaware of what had happened to time today. Nobody but Henry and me had noticed anything at all.

I could understand why I was aware of the slowdown and immune to its effects: I was part of the process that had caused it, part of the "three-in-one." My connection to the clock had kept me outside the slowdown I helped it create. But why hadn't Henry been trapped in the slowdown like the rest of the world?

I was baffled, sitting tensely on my bed, the closet door firmly closed.

I was also worried about Crutchley. Why had Aunt Ruth suddenly decided to talk to them herself, in private, instead of using me to avoid them?

Had they promised her something she didn't want me to know about?

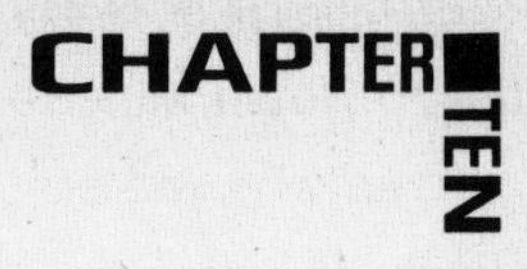

I couldn't concentrate on anything in school the next morning. Everything gnawed at me like Pandora's unleashed evils. Part of me felt horribly guilty for betraying Uncle Marco by telling Henry about the boxes. How could I ever make up for it? Uncle Marco would probably never forgive me.

But another part of me kept my eyes on the clock, counting the minutes until lunch, when I could talk to Henry. How could I *not* have told him? He was the only other person who had shared that terrifying, unbelievable experience with me. He was my passport to sanity—if it weren't for him, I would have to be crazy. We had to discuss it, compare notes—and try to understand why it had happened to Henry, too, and not just me.

I spotted him just as I was entering the cafeteria. He was coming in through the opposite doorway, tall and thin in black jeans and a faded blue sweat shirt. Across the large room, our eyes locked. We hurried toward each other, ignoring the kids moving back and forth between us, not moving our eyes from each other's faces.

When we reached each other, we clasped our hands together, not thinking about the other kids.

"Are you hungry?" Henry asked me.

I shook my head.

"Then let's get out of here."

We passed Linda and Jeff waiting in the lunch line. "Where are you two going?" Linda wanted to know, sounding like she was accusing us of something.

Henry didn't let me answer. "We have an errand. Can't cover for you today. See you later," he said quickly, not stopping. He pulled me forward before they could ask any more questions—and before I had a chance to give in and do what they wanted me to do. This was a purposeful side to Henry that I hadn't been aware of before.

"Yesterday, at school and at band and on the way home," he said as we made our way out of the noisy cafeteria, "everything was slow, right?"

I nodded.

"But it didn't seem huge, impossible," he went on. "It was more kind of like the feeling you have when you're sick, with a fever or something, kind of dizzy, out of it. Is that the way you felt?"

"Yes," I said, nodding again.

The auditorium was across the hall from the cafeteria. It was often locked, but Henry dropped my hand and tried the door anyway. Today it opened.

We peered inside. There were some folding chairs on the stage, but the place seemed to be empty for the moment. Henry ushered me into the high-ceilinged, dimly lit space, down the sloping aisle to the middle. We slid into the first two seats in a row.

He was still talking. "But then, after I got home, then it got . . ." He lifted his hands, unable to express the enormity of it. "Like, everything just *stopped*."

I thought of something. "What about that car that was following us? Did it keep after you all the way home?"

"No." He looked worried. "It stopped and waited in front of your house. Didn't you notice?"

"No. A lot of other things were going on."

"Another one was waiting in front of my house when I got home. I pointed it out to my mother before she left. Maybe I shouldn't have."

"Why not?"

"They might be thinking of selling."

"Funny," I said. "Aunt Ruth wanted to talk to Crutchley herself yesterday. She usually avoids them. Maybe she's giving in, too."

He sighed. "But that's not what we're talking about now. Lucky thing Mom left before it started!" He shook his head, his eyes wide.

"What do you mean?"

"When my folks got home, they hadn't noticed anything—just like everybody else. So if they'd been at home when everything stopped except you and me, how do you think *I* would have looked to them?"

This had not occurred to me. "I guess . . . it would have looked to them like you were a blur, flashing around like lightning. Wow."

"You were alone, too, right? Or else you'd be in some kind of trouble."

"Yeah, I was alone—sort of. I mean, at least there were no other people there. It was a good thing." I paused. "It's funny, but for some reason I don't *want* anybody else to know." I coughed nervously. "I mean, two people, so we know we're not going crazy. That's enough."

He took my hand again and squeezed it. My first impulse was to pull it away. But the way he was suddenly smiling now was so infectious that I didn't take my hand away; I squeezed back. We just sat there grinning at each other, like we were the only two people in the world. In a way, we were. And even though I was scared about everything that was happening, I still couldn't help feeling good about Henry at that moment—real good.

He looked away, releasing my hand, and cleared his throat. "But time is normal now, as far as I can tell," he said. "The bell won't wait. What were you telling me on the phone yesterday, about the boxes doing it?" He seemed reluctant to ask. Maybe he was afraid to risk breaking the good feeling between us by finding out I was crazy after all.

I felt guilty about Uncle Marco, but what choice did I have? Henry was the only person I could turn to. And so I told him everything that had happened yesterday afternoon—and how time had ground to a stop just after the delivery I made.

Henry stared at me, looking pale in the dim auditorium light. "This is for real, Annie?" he finally said.

"How could I make *up* something that crazy?" I asked him. "Anyway, is it any more unbelievable than what you saw with your own eyes?"

He thought for a moment. "No, I guess not. Gee, that's a lot for you to be dealing with," he said with concern. "I've got to see the boxes. Then we can both share all of it."

"Okay, Henry." I didn't feel so guilty about Uncle Marco now. I just felt lucky that Henry really was such a nice guy. "I think it's good that we're in this together, but I have to say, I don't understand why. I mean, why is it happening to you and not just me? You got any ideas?"

The bell rang. Henry got up. "No. But I'll think about it. We can talk more after school."

I couldn't avoid Linda, who sat next to me in English. "So what was that all about?" she said as we were sitting down. "Skipping lunch? With *Henry*?" I had told her before that I didn't like Henry the way he liked me.

I didn't know what to say.

Then I thought of a subject I knew Linda wouldn't want to hear about—I was beginning to understand her, finally. "It's a problem I'm having about something Uncle Marco left me. I didn't think you'd be interested. But Henry was. If only you knew how much I miss Uncle Marco! Want me to tell you—"

Miss Rothschild started to talk and Linda turned away. I could see her mentally rolling her eyes. I smiled to myself.

"Nobody following us today," Henry said after we'd gone a few blocks from school. "What does that mean?"

"Did your parents say anything to you about Crutchley?" I asked him. "Aunt Ruth kept her phone call a secret from me."

"They didn't. But they're hiding something. I can tell."

I nodded unhappily as we walked through the stone gate to our neighborhood. What would happen if Aunt Ruth sold the house to Crutchley and they tore it down? I loved the house. And without it, would Uncle Marco ever come back? What would happen to the boxes, which were more powerful than anyone would believe? The clock would do something terrible to the world if they tried to wreck the house; I could feel it.

I looked around at the big bare trees and the frozen lawns, the imposing brick and stone houses. It was beautiful here in a way that could never be replaced. The world already had more than enough malls.

"Aunt Ruth came home early yesterday," I told Henry as I let him inside the house. It was just after three now. "She usually doesn't come back until five-thirty, but who knows what she's going to do anymore? She's checking on me. So we better hurry."

Still, Henry stopped briefly to look around. "Great house," he murmured. "I love the stairway and the stained glass window."

I took him down to the basement first. Halfway down the steps he jolted, then stopped. "Huh?" he said in the darkness, sounding scared.

"You're not going crazy," I said. "I told you, you can only understand them inside your head. ESP. Come on."

At the bottom I reached up automatically and pulled on the light. Henry looked shaky, confused. "They're over here in the root cellar," I said.

As we approached, the sonar and alien voices filled my head. But I had no awareness of any sensations from Henry's mind. *Henry?* I projected. *Hey, Henry? It's Annie. This is the real me.*

There was no response. It seemed that the ESP worked only between humans and the creatures, but not between humans. I have to admit I was a little disappointed—naturally I was curious to know what Henry was thinking.

But I had been curious about the boxes, too, and look what had happened. It might be better not to know exactly what was going on inside another person's head.

"Be sure to bow just like I do when you see them," I whispered to Henry. "They don't like it if you don't greet them right."

I hadn't been down here since the beginning of the slowdown yesterday. Even before entering the root cellar I could sense that something was very different in there. "Wait. Don't come in yet," I whispered to Henry. I squeezed through the left-hand side of the doorway—the rest of it seemed to be blocked—and reached up and turned on the light.

I gasped and put my hand over my mouth. Henry slipped inside tentatively and stood beside me, gaping.

The structure almost filled the room, floor to ceiling; there were only a few feet of space for Henry and me to stand in.

The grid of yesterday must have merely been scaffolding. The building now revealed was far more complex. It was entirely glittering black—the creatures could not perceive color, after all. But clearly their sonar made them aware of the shape of things. Sharp conical spires spiked around the steeply sloped roof, and beneath these were colonnaded hallways, small and simple at the top—for the lower classes, I imagined—and growing more spacious and ornate as rampways, first narrow, then wider, descended toward the bottom. The two lower stories were elaborately carved with statues of monstrous creatures, not like anything on earth—many-limbed, with fangs and claws. The statues looked nothing like the creatures who had built this palace in my basement. In the middle of the structure a large arched opening rose from the floor to the third level, which seemed to go all the way through to the wall behind it.

Henry looked at me, then back to the structure, his mouth open. "They started this . . . when?" he breathed.

"The first time I saw it was yesterday. And then it was nothing but . . . a scaffold. All this happened during the slowdown yesterday. I haven't been down here since then. The slowdown speeded up construction like crazy. According to a normal clock, they built this palace in an *hour.*"

"Is this a dream, or what?" Henry murmured.

"You know it's real. Do you believe me now? About how these creatures, and me, and mainly the clock in my closet upstairs, all three together, were what made the slowdown?"

He nodded wordlessly.

I hadn't greeted any of the creatures yet because so far they were paying no attention to us at all. Some of them were crowded around a very tall and peculiar object on the floor just in front of the building. Two slightly inclining posts, three stories high, were joined by a carved crossbeam at the top. Attached to the crossbeam by long cables was something like a boat. Four of the small, blotched creatures—the lowest class—rode in the boat, pumping their bodies backward and forward to make it swing as high as possible in a tremendous arc.

They were imaginative, I had to give them that.

The crowd on the ground, those with the best view, were sleek and plump, waving their front legs, and in my head I could hear the equivalent of cheers and boos. Others watched from the colonnades of the building; the higher they were, and therefore the worse the view, the smaller and sicklier they looked.

The riders in the boat were working very hard. The boat swung higher now, more than 180 degrees. And then, at the top of its arc, two of the creatures tumbled out, smashing down onto the floor. They wriggled and spasmed as the swing slowed. Some other small ones carried the wounded ones away. Meanwhile, the sleek ones on the ground rubbed their front legs together with each other. I felt no wave of alarm or regret this time, only excitement and suspense.

"It almost seems like they were betting on the outcome or something," Henry said, still whispering. "Like this swing thing is all a game to them."

"Yeah . . ." I said. "And to think how sorry I felt about the ones who were sacrificed yesterday." I shook my head. "They're obviously intelligent. And yet—"

Greetings, one of the sleek ones on the floor addressed me, bowing.

I nudged Henry and thought *Greetings* and bowed back. Henry imitated me.

An unpleasantly startled reaction popped inside my head. *There is another foreigner here. Why are there two of you? Only the nervous system is allowed! No one else in this world is to know! This is very dangerous! You have disobeyed. When the Lord knows this, you will be punished. Severely punished. This is not—*

Oddly, I wasn't scared—not of this thing, anyway. What could these creatures do to me? And what could the clock find out if I didn't tell it? I was the only means of communication between them, after all.

For the first time, I felt an electric tingle of power. Quiet, obedient Annie, everybody else's messenger, had made the world stop. Now I was the nervous system, in charge of the messages. It was incredibly exciting. I could tell the clock whatever I wanted; I could control everything. I didn't have to just obey *these* things.

I was also annoyed at their attitude. *But isn't this my house you're in?* I interrupted it. *And how have I disobeyed? Nobody ever told me not to do this.*

The creature was twisting its front legs together like a person wringing her hands. *And we don't understand why we are aware of communication from the other foreigner. You, nervous system, are the only foreigner we are supposed to be able to understand. Something is wrong. Something is very, very wrong.*

You didn't think I knew that already? But I don't really think it's me who's in the wrong. I think maybe it might be you who's—

You must tell the Lord right away, it commanded me. *And you must also tell it what our home is like now, in all details. Study it hard, and remember. The Lord will be very eager to see how much we accomplished during the slowdown. The Lord will be very happy about the swing ritual and the two more who are sacrificed to the Lord's goodness. Go! Now! And take the other foreigner with you, away from here, up to the mercy of the Lord. Tell the Lord about the terrible transgression you have committed.*

"Huh?" Henry said, turning to me, looking very uncomfortable.

"You heard all that?"

"I sure did. They seem to have something against me." He wiped his forehead. "Annie, this is weird."

"Yeah. And wait'll you see . . ." I turned back to the creature. *Who said you could boss me around like that? If you want me to help you, I expect you to be polite about it.*

For a moment, it couldn't seem to think of a response. Then it bowed to me, more deeply than ever.

Okay. That's better. We'll go now. And even though you were rude, I still have to tell you how beautiful your home is. It's not just a home; it's a palace. I will picture it for the

Lord. I will picture the two who died in your . . . ritual. And I'm sure the Lord will understand that I must have help. I can't be the nervous system all alone. It's too much.

I turned back to Henry. He could hear what they were thinking at me, but not what I was thinking at them. "I told it I would do what it said, but that I need you—I can't do it on my own. Come on, let's get out of here. I want to show you the clock upstairs; they call it the Lord. It's what slowed down time yesterday so they could build this so fast. Don't forget to bow."

We both bowed to the creature, which returned the gesture again—perfunctorily this time, it seemed to me—and then we squeezed out of the root cellar.

There was a creak on the basement stairway—or was it a footstep? "Did you hear that?" I said to Henry, alarmed.

He shrugged. "Sure. A creak. Our house always creaks. Doesn't yours?"

"I guess so," I said. But the sound bothered me. Had I locked the front door? I might have forgotten, preoccupied with letting Henry inside.

In the front hall I checked the door. It opened. "I forgot to lock the door," I said. "What if somebody sneaked in?" I turned the lock and pushed and pulled on the door to make sure.

"Who would want to sneak—" Henry started to say. He didn't finish. I knew we were both thinking Crutchley.

"Well, it's too late now," I said. "If somebody was here,

they already had the chance to get out without you and me seeing." I sighed as we started up the stairs.

"You're imagining it, Annie," Henry tried to reassure me. "If somebody was really watching and listening down there, I would have known it."

I stopped at the top of the stairs. "Now I have to decide whether to tell the clock about you or not," I said. "Those things downstairs, I don't see how they can punish me. I mean, they're not exactly kindhearted, but they're little, and polite sometimes, and gullible. The clock is what I'm really afraid of."

"Afraid of a clock?"

"Wait'll you see it."

"But won't it be able to tell I'm with you, like they did?"

"I don't know. They really need me to communicate with it. That's why they call me the nervous system. It's possible the clock might know only what I tell it."

Henry was shaking his head again. "If I hadn't seen what I did yesterday, if I hadn't seen what's down in your basement, I'd think . . ." He grimaced and shrugged his shoulders. "I don't know what I'd think."

"Come see the clock," I said. "I don't know if it'll know you're there or not. Try not to think too hard, okay?"

"How do you not think too hard?"

Outside the door of my room I put my finger to my lips. "Just try to keep calm, unemotional," I whispered. "Don't project your thoughts or anything. Maybe it won't know you're there. Maybe I can figure out if it cares." I stepped inside the room and he followed. Henry stood back as I opened the closet door.

The clock wasn't moving quickly as it had been yesterday during the slowdown. It sat there, the propellers just above the level of the box, the tendrils now draped over the edge. As I watched, it moved a notch, and clicked, and was silent again.

I nodded at Henry and moved to the side. He stepped to the closet door and looked in. For a long moment he just stared. I couldn't read his expression. We turned and looked silently at each other. Then I focused my attention back on the clock.

The palace in the basement is finished—and that's what it is, a palace. I pictured it in as much solid detail as I could. *They are hoping you will be pleased with how much they accomplished during the slowdown you gave them. They are also hoping you will be pleased about this.* I relived the ritual of the swing in my brain, playing it for the clock like a movie, ending with the two deaths.

I waited. Nothing happened. *They are not asking for anything now,* I continued. *I guess . . . I guess they just want to know if you are pleased with their efforts—and what you want them to do next.*

Again, I waited.

A tendril lashed out with lightning speed and fastened itself to Henry's cheek. We both screamed. Henry ripped it away from his face. It made a tearing sound, leaving a nasty red welt. Tears of pain sprang to Henry's eyes. We stumbled backward away from the closet.

And bumped into somebody who went "oomph" and crashed to the floor. We spun around. A very tall man in a black turtleneck and a quilted, military-style jacket was jumping to his feet. His hair was crew cut; he had a small video camera around his neck.

Before Henry or I could react, the man was out of the room and running lightly down the stairs. The front door slammed. From the window, we watched him jump into a familiar dark car, which rapidly sped out of sight.

CHAPTER ELEVEN

Henry's hand was on his cheek. "Geez, this hurts," he said, breathing hard. "And how did that guy get in here, anyway?"

My heart was pounding. "I told you. I forgot to lock the door. And then I thought I heard footsteps. He must have been from . . ."

We didn't have to say it.

"Maybe they noticed something funny when they were watching our houses yesterday—like seeing us inside, running past the windows like a blur," Henry said slowly.

"I went past the windows a lot. And today they decided to investigate."

"I was at the windows a lot, too, in the slowdown," I said. "I wonder how much he saw today?"

"Whatever he saw, he got pictures of it." Henry took his hand away from his cheek. "Do you think this might be poisoned or something?" he said, his voice hoarse. "That *thing* in your closet doesn't like me any better than the ones downstairs. It really is a lot worse, like you said."

"I just don't get it," I said, shaking my head, bewildered.

"Don't get what?"

"Why didn't the clock freeze you in the slowdown like everybody else? Could it be because you knew it existed? You and I and the creatures are the only ones who know. And maybe whoever *knows* about the clock doesn't get stuck in the slowdown. Would that do it?"

"Don't ask me about its motives. Just get me to a mirror. I want to see what it did to me. How bad does it look?"

"Not too bad. Like a burn or something. The bathroom's this way."

While Henry studied his wound in the bathroom mirror, I surreptitiously checked my watch. I didn't want him to think I wasn't concerned about him, but I had to be careful about Aunt Ruth coming home. It was only 3:35. I doubted that Aunt Ruth would leave the bank early two days in a row—she loved bossing people around there so much—but I still had to be careful. It would be a disaster if she got home and Henry was here.

I found some antiseptic ointment and cleaned and put the stuff on his wound while he sat on the toilet seat. "Feel better?"

"Uh-huh." He nodded gratefully. "Thanks, Annie." He looked away. "I think I better go now, in case your aunt comes back. And I need to think about all this."

I could understand why he wanted to get away from here. But, oddly, I didn't feel as uncomfortable about the clock as I had before.

"Be sure to lock it," he said to me at the door.

"I'll never forget again."

"Don't look so worried, Annie," he said, forcing a wan smile. "We'll figure out how to deal with this. There's got to be some way."

"I hope so." I locked the door carefully when he left.

I didn't know what to tell Aunt Ruth. I couldn't tell her about Henry being here and I couldn't tell her about the boxes. But I wanted to tell her about the man who had snuck inside with a camera. Crutchley had to be behind it, and she needed to know about it, so she would understand what crooks they were. I didn't like the way she was dealing with them secretly now.

She came home at the normal time, 5:30, but she was in an abnormally good mood. "Anne! Come down here right away. I want to talk to you!" she brayed upstairs at me as soon as she slammed the door.

I hurried down. How was I going to tell her about the spy from Crutchley without giving anything away?

"Something big just happened, right before I left the bank," she said, rubbing her hands together and chuckling wheezily. "And by *big* what I mean is: big bucks!" She was actually almost smiling, which was unusual for her, though I could also see the twitching effort she was making to keep the smile from getting out of control.

My heart sank. I was pretty sure what she was going to say. But I didn't want to put any words into her mouth. "What . . . happened?"

"Aren't you excited? You look about as happy as a wet dishrag." She shrugged her fat arms out of her coat and let it fall onto the built-in oak window seat.

I forced a smile. "Please tell me the good news, Aunt Ruth," I said.

"Crutchley made me an offer I can't refuse. I knew holding out was the right strategy." She was gloating, mentally patting herself on the back. "You want to know how much they offered?" She leaned closer to me, really smiling now, showing her teeth. I decided her habitual scowl was more attractive. "Guess, Anne! Guess how much they offered!"

"How . . . how should I know?" I said.

She was practically slobbering now, she was so excited. "Guess, Anne!" she ordered me.

The last offer they had made, when I was screening the calls for Aunt Ruth, was $280,000. "I don't know," I said. "Uh . . . three hundred thousand dollars?"

Aunt Ruth threw back her head and roared. "You think

I'd sell for a pittance like that?" she managed to say, gasping. "*I'm* not dumb. *I* know what this house is worth." She pressed her lips together and began to hum, looking so smug I wanted to smack her.

"I hope you didn't agree to anything, sign anything with them, Aunt Ruth," I forced myself to say. I knew Aunt Ruth didn't want to hear this; it would infuriate her. But I had to tell her; I had to try to change her mind. "I've been trying to tell you, Crutchley's crooked. It's not just that they want to tear down this historic area and build a horrible mall. They were following Henry, they were following me, in a threatening way." I took a deep breath and pushed the words out. "And today . . . somebody got into the house. I forgot to lock the door, and some guy got in here, taking pictures. When I saw him, he ran away. Who else could he be from but Crutchley? You want to sell the house to people who—"

Her smile, predictably, had faded. "You ungrateful brat!" she interrupted me. "After all my planning, and plotting, and strategizing, and being a sharp bargainer—all for your future—and then it works because I carried it off, and all you can do is give me this . . . this *environmental* garbage, or whatever, and talk about your paranoid fantasies." She lifted her hands. "It's too much! It's just *too much!*" She turned away from me.

It was pointless to try to persuade her of anything. It had never been possible to reason with her. "Sorry, Aunt Ruth.

How much? Please tell me how much they offered. I'm dying to know." In a morbid way, I was.

She swung back to me, her face lighting up again. "One . . . million . . . bucks," she said triumphantly.

My stomach tightened into a hard, cold ball. "A *million*?" I said, very softly. Why had they tripled their offer? Had they seen enough yesterday and today so that they understood what was really going on and what the clock could do?

The phone rang. "If it's Crutchley, I'll talk to them," Aunt Ruth said. "If it's anybody else, I'm not home. And if it's one of your little friends, get off quick. And don't breathe a word about that figure, not to anybody. They're not paying anybody else that much. It's only because of my brilliant business sense that I got them up that high. Hurry up, answer it!"

"Annie?" Henry said.

"Yeah."

"My parents are selling." He was talking softly, but breathing hard. "Crutchley offered them a million dollars."

"Yeah. Same here" was all I could say.

"You can't say anything because of your aunt. I get it. But it just happened a few minutes ago. It *has* to be because of what they saw yesterday and today. They're smart. They must understand about that clock, and they want it, really bad. And they're interested in me and you, too. Your aunt tell you that?"

"No."

"Hurry up, Anne! We have things to talk about!" Aunt Ruth bellowed.

"Try to stop her from signing anything. Stall. Whatever," Henry said. "We'll think of a plan. Gotta go."

"See you tomorrow," I said, and put down the phone.

"Who was that?" Aunt Ruth demanded.

"Just Linda. Only person who ever calls me."

"You sounded pretty secretive."

"She just has a message she wants me to give to a friend, that's all. Anyway"—I tried to sound cheerful—"tell me more."

"Funny thing was, they asked me about *you*," she said. "Of course, they know who you are because of all the times I told you not to let them talk to me." Again, she smiled a little, as though hiding from them had been a clever ploy on her part. Then she remembered what she was saying, and the smile sagged. "But I don't know why they have any interest in you, and for some reason they didn't want to tell me. But they want to talk to you—and the other kid whose parents were also holding out—before we sign the purchase and sale." She frowned at me, an expression I was a lot more familiar with. "What is this, Anne? This interest in *you*? It's the one sour note in the whole deal."

What could I say? I shrugged and lifted my hands. "I don't know, Aunt Ruth. Honest. All I know about Crutchley is the times I talked to them on the phone, when they were rude. And the times they followed me and Henry—the other kid whose parents held out. And the time today when one of their spies sneaked in here. I don't know why they would be interested in me or—"

Aunt Ruth peered closer, squinting. "What's this about a spy? I seem to remember you mentioning that a little while ago."

"Uh, this strange man got into the house today. It was my fault because I forgot to lock the door." In a way, I was relieved that Crutchley hadn't said anything about this to Aunt Ruth—they might have told her Henry was here. "He was sneaking around with a video camera. When I saw him, he ran out. He had to be from Crutchley. Who else would be interested?"

Aunt Ruth's face darkened. "You were an idiot to forget to lock the door. And I don't like people sneaking into my house."

"That's what I was trying to say. You want to do business with people who use tactics like *that*?"

"For a million dollars, I'm not sure I care what tactics they use. I can see why they'd want to get in here to get a true idea of the house's value. I just don't understand what their interest is in you, that's all." She suddenly thrust her head at me. "Are you hiding something? I've had this funny feeling ever since your uncle left."

It was probably too late to make any difference, but somehow, in my gut, I still didn't want Aunt Ruth to know about the boxes. "What would I be hiding?" I said, unhappy and confused. "And why would that have anything to do with Crutchley?"

She sniffed, though it was more like a snort. "Well, we'll see what happens tomorrow, after the meeting."

"Meeting?"

"They want to talk to you and the other kid. What's his name?"

"Henry."

"Yeah. I don't get it. But they want to talk to you two. I don't like it. But for a million dollars . . ." Suddenly she thrust her head at me again. "You wouldn't do anything to try to queer this deal, would you?" she said threateningly. "I can tell you have something against it, for some immature adolescent reason of your own that I swear I will *never* understand. But just let me tell you one thing: If this deal doesn't happen, your precious uncle is not getting another *penny* of that annuity. And then where will he be, huh?"

He'd be in big trouble. Uncle Marco was always very careful about money. He didn't seem to make any from his travels—they had some other, unknown purpose. He depended completely on his inheritance, which was doled out to him annually by the bank. Without it, he'd have to stop carrying out his important missions and get some sort of ordinary job. I knew that would kill him.

Aunt Ruth lifted her head, displaying all her chins, and waddled over to the TV.

CHAPTER TWELVE

The next day, Thursday, Henry and I met with Crutchley Development after school.

It was arranged the night before. Henry's parents didn't understand it, and neither did Aunt Ruth, and the three of them didn't like it at all. But Crutchley was in control. Their offer of a million dollars put the ball in their court. And Crutchley wanted to see Henry and me, no one else, at their offices.

The auditorium was locked at lunch that day. Henry and I whispered in the library. "Okay, Henry. I want you to be totally honest," I said. "I mean, a million dollars would change your life. Maybe you don't care so much about the clock, and Uncle Marco, and saving the neighborhood. I don't blame you. Don't pretend you're on my side just to be nice."

"I'm nice, but I'm not that nice." Henry smiled. "If I wanted the million dollars, I'd want it, for sure. But what will it mean? We'll move into some boring modern house. We'll have nicer cars. I'll maybe go to a private school and an Ivy League college." He shrugged. "Who needs it? Especially when you think about the alternative."

"Yeah, well, if Aunt Ruth got a million dollars, I'd never see a penny of it anyway. Not that I really care. It's like you said—consider the alternative and nothing else matters. What does Crutchley think is going on?"

"They must have seen and heard enough to get an idea of what the clock can do," Henry said, very serious now. "Wow, could a development company ever use something like that! They'd have our houses wrecked and that mall built in days. If they didn't believe it, they wouldn't make that kind of offer—only hours after the spy got into your house."

"So what are we going to do? I mean, we can't just tell them! It has to be a secret." I twisted my hands together. "It just keeps getting worse and worse. I can't stand this! I don't know how I can even go there. Maybe I can pretend I'm sick or—"

"That would just be putting it off. We have to get it over with."

"But what are we going to do?" Suddenly I was close to tears.

"The only thing we can do is play dumb and wait," Henry said. "We don't admit to anything; we don't *know* anything. It all has to come from them."

"But then what? What if they really do know what's going on? Then what do we do?"

"I don't know." Henry looked grim. "Maybe we just go on playing dumb. Deny everything. Make it look like their spies made it up. Try to convince them nothing unusual is happening."

"But if that works, and they take their million dollars away, Aunt Ruth will kill Uncle Marco's annuity—and then she'll kill me. I mean it, Henry. That's what she's like. If she killed me, I wouldn't be one bit surprised."

"No, you wouldn't be. You'd be dead," Henry said, with a trace of a smile. "Anyway, what would be worse: Uncle Marco losing his annuity and you getting killed? Or Crutchley getting the clock?"

"Crutchley getting the clock," I said instantly. "Nothing would be worse than that. Think how fast they could wreck everything beautiful in the world."

"Exactly." Henry looked hard at me and took a deep breath. "Just keep that in mind, whatever happens. Never forget it."

On the way out of the library he thought of something else. "And don't act scared. We're confused; we have no idea why we're there. But we're not scared. If they know we're scared, they'll know we're hiding something."

"If I can act like I'm not scared, they should give me an Oscar," I muttered.

One of the sleek dark cars with smoked windows that had followed us was waiting for us after school. The back door lock clicked open as we approached it. Henry gave me a look of encouragement, then pulled open the door and slid inside. I followed him, feeling colder inside the car than outside in mid-January.

The driver, a young man in a dark suit and dark glasses, nodded at us but said nothing. Was he one of the drivers who had followed us? He accelerated smoothly away from the school. Soon we were on the highway heading down-town.

For twenty minutes, Henry and I sat in uncomfortable silence, aware of the driver and also the fact that the car might be bugged.

Downtown, the driver stopped in front of a shiny glass skyscraper. "Thirty-ninth floor," he said. "They're expecting you."

The elevator swept us up there in seconds; my leaden stomach sank to my knees. We stepped off into a foyer: modern couches and a high plastic counter with a recep-tionist sitting behind it. Above her head, "Crutchley Development" gleamed in big chrome letters. The whole floor belonged to them.

The receptionist's face was a mask of makeup; her hair swooped back in plastic-like curves. "Can I help you?" she said without expression.

"We have an appointment," Henry said. "Anne Levi and Henry Vail."

"Just a moment, please." Long fingernails clicked on an invisible keyboard. "Take a seat and someone will be right out," she said.

We perched uncomfortably on one of the nubbly couches; I was afraid my coat might get snow or dust on the upholstery. "This is what it would feel like to live in a million-dollar house," Henry whispered. Trying to shush him, I showed him a magazine called *International Development*, which had a picture of an exotic tropical resort on the cover, with pools and thatched-roofed bungalows and little artificial waterfalls. "I wonder how many poor fishermen got their livelihoods taken away from them to make room for that stupid place?" Henry said.

Before I had a chance to shush him again, a genial voice said, "Probably quite a few."

We both looked up guiltily. An elderly white-haired man in an expensive suit stood there smiling down at us from beneath his immaculately groomed white mustache. "And now those poor fishermen have enough money, in their community, so they don't have to work like slaves in the hot sun hauling nets from dawn to dark to make a few pennies," he continued. He cleared his throat and extended his hand. "Adam Crutchley. Nice to meet you."

We were important, for sure—this guy had to be the owner of the company. We got up awkwardly and shook his hand. "This way, please," he said and ushered us through an opening to the left of the receptionist. "Did you have a comfortable ride?" he asked us.

We were walking along the edge of a very large room filled with desks in cubicles. Everything was pale purple and chrome. Inside every cubicle was a person and a computer and a phone.

"Sure, real comfortable, thanks," Henry said. "The car looked a little bit familiar—"

I glared at him. He should know better than to start out making accusations. We were supposed to play dumb.

"Excuse me. A little bit what?" Crutchley said.

"Uh, fancy, I was going to say," Henry corrected himself as we stepped out of the big room into a luxurious marble-floored anteroom. And I was thinking: The farther we get from the elevator, the harder it's going to be to get out of here.

"Well, nothing but the best for you two." Crutchley beamed at us. We followed him across the elegant room. "Right in here, please." He pushed open a polished wooden door and gestured us inside.

The first thing I saw was the view. One whole wall of

glass jutted out, so that you almost felt as if you were falling through it. There was the winter city at twilight, with only the tops of the skyscrapers reflecting the brilliant orange sunset. The barren black-and-white parks, the frozen, winding river were already in shadow; the many bridges glittered with lights. The whole metropolis was framed, enclosed by this window, as if it were the property of Crutchley Development.

Crutchley was pointing. "Way over there on the left, where you just see trees and some roofs. That's our new site—your old neighborhood."

Henry stiffened beside me. I touched his elbow to stop him from saying anything.

"Anne Levi and Henry Vail," Crutchley said, turning to face the people seated at the table. "This is my son, Denham Crutchley."

A flabby, dark-haired man with a greasy face smiled stiffly at us.

"The head of our legal department, Danielle Korngold."

She had short red hair and was dressed all in chic black. She nodded briskly, her sharp blue eyes assessing us.

"Director of operations, Brad Whelpley."

This man had a blond crew cut and a pockmarked face; he wore a jacket and a denim shirt and no tie. He looked like an ex-Marine. He lifted one corner of his mouth and winked.

"And Ms. MacElberg, my executive secretary."

She was a skinny middle-aged woman with her dark hair in a low bun, wearing a green suit. Her fingers were poised over a laptop.

"Sit down, sit down," Crutchley said to us, pulling out two chairs at the end of the table opposite from everyone else. "Refreshments? Soft drinks?"

We looked around. Nobody else had anything. "No, thanks," we said together.

Crutchley walked down the room and sat at the head of the table, across from us, surrounded by his cronies. He folded his manicured hands on the expensive wood. "And now . . . What can we do for you two today?" he asked us.

Henry and I looked at each other. We didn't have to pretend to be mystified. "What can *you* do for *us*?" Henry murmured.

Crutchley was still smiling pleasantly. The others watched us. "Yes, that's what I said," Crutchley answered him.

"Well, you could tell us why you . . . *invited* us here," Henry said. He made it clear, by his tone of voice, that it hadn't been an invitation—it had been an order.

"We just wanted to have a nice little chat and talk about what kind of goodies you'd like after your folks sign the purchase and sale agreements."

Did they think we were babies or what? "Goodies?" Henry said, sounding confused.

"I guess you're too young for cars." Crutchley looked at Danielle Korngold, the lawyer. She nodded almost imperceptibly—she had already done her research on us. Crutchley smiled back at us and lifted his arms like a TV evangelist. "But you're not too young for clothes—wardrobes of designer clothes. You're not too young for trips—to Disney World or other wonderful parks. Or how about Hollywood? Universal Studios is a big favorite. You'd impress those movie people in your new outfits."

Henry and I looked at each other again. I could tell he wanted to make gagging noises, like I did. What kind of imbeciles did this jerk think we were, anyway? "But—we still don't know why you're offering us these things," Henry said. "We do know you offered a million dollars for our houses. Do developers usually buy presents for the kids, too?" He was amazing; he sounded genuinely naive.

Crutchley chuckled uncomfortably. "Well, no, not usually." He glanced around at the others, as if unsure about how to proceed. "But you two are special."

"Your little toys," Danielle Korngold said, resting her chin on her folded, red-nailed hands and smiling sweetly at me. "We think they're just really terrific."

"Toys?" I said, trying to keep the tremor out of my voice so I would sound dumb and not scared.

There was a silence. Nobody seemed to know what to say. Outside the window the cold, glowing buildings were fading as the last of the sunlight sank away.

"Oh, come on, let's just get to the point," said Brad Whelpley, the director of operations with the crew cut and the acne scars. He let his eyes flick back and forth between Henry and me. "We're very interested in that stunt you pulled off Tuesday afternoon. When you speeded yourselves up—and that construction in your basement was finished in no time. We need that capability. We need it a lot."

My stomach went cold. They did know.

At least this Whelpley guy wasn't treating us like idiots. But we still had to act stupid. "I . . . I don't understand," Henry said. He turned to me. "Do you know what he means, Annie?"

I shook my head.

"Oh, for Pete's sake!" Whelpley said, tapping the table with his fist and looking around at the others, then back at us. "You kids can't get away with this. You're just wasting our time. We have evidence."

"Evidence?" Henry said, wide-eyed.

Crutchley didn't look so genial anymore—clearly he was used to getting his own way. "Turn around," he said to us. He gestured impatiently behind him. Dark curtains gathered across the window, and the lights went out. We turned around to see a screen sliding down from the ceiling on the wall behind us.

A picture appeared on the screen: Henry's turreted stone house, late afternoon. It was dark, but you could make out the pine trees moving slightly past the stars in the wind. I could barely see a shadowy, gargoyle-like carved figure crouched under the turret. But the windows were brightly lit.

A blur flashed past a window on the second floor. It was so startling and unexpected that I couldn't help jerking in my seat. The camera zoomed in on the window and the shape flashed past it again, going the other way, larger but still too fast to see. It was even more unnerving the second time.

Then the quality of the picture became grainier; the trees stopped moving: slow motion. This time the figure took at least a second to move into the window, stop and look outside, and then slide away. If you watched closely, Henry's face was just barely recognizable.

The picture switched to my house. Like Henry, I zipped almost invisibly past the window a couple of times before the cameraman slowed it down enough so that you could see it was me.

"Gee, what funny pictures," Henry said in the darkness. "That's a cool trick camera. Maybe you could give me something like *that.*"

I found his hand and squeezed it. Hopeless as it seemed, he was still fighting them.

The general sigh was audible from the other end of the table. "Take a look at these trick shots, sweetie," a woman's voice said—it had to be the lawyer, Danielle Korngold.

Now the picture swam up behind two people—Henry and me in the basement, looking at the black palace and the creatures who had built it. "All this happened during the slowdown yesterday," I was saying. "I haven't been down here since then. The slowdown speeded up construction like crazy. According to a normal clock, they built this palace in an *hour.*"

"Is this a dream, or what?" Henry murmured.

"You know it's real," I said, and I wanted to cringe as I heard the words. "Do you believe me now? About how these creatures, and me, and mainly the clock in my closet upstairs, all three together, were what made the slowdown?"

Another picture, Henry and me from behind again, but more brightly lit. The cameraman managed to get a good shot of the clock face over our shoulders. The tendril lashed out. Henry and I screamed and backed into the camera, and the screen went blank.

The lights came on; the screen slid up into the ceiling. Our eyes met for only an instant as we turned to face the others. Did I look as pale as Henry did?

Danielle Korngold was smiling sweetly again. "Trick shots, is that what you're going to say this time?" she said. "Pretty good trick camera that can put words into people's mouths."

Neither of us could think of anything to say.

"You understand," Crutchley said to us, not smiling now, his voice gravelly, "the gifts we're offering you are not to persuade you to give us anything or help us out. We'll get what we need ourselves. The gifts are more a reminder for you to keep quiet—this capability of speeding up construction has to be exclusively ours. We already know your parents and guardian don't know anything about it; we made sure to find that out. So the gifts we're offering are a nice little reminder to you to say nothing to anybody. We'd like to keep things pleasant."

And hanging in the air was the implied threat: If we *didn't* accept these gifts and keep quiet, then things might not be so pleasant after that.

"If the gifts are just to keep us quiet, then you're wasting your money," Henry said. He shrugged. "We still don't understand what there is for us to tell anybody."

"You saw the videos!" Whelpley snapped.

"A trick camera," Henry said. He sounded calm but I could see from his eyes that he was really scared.

"But she said it in so many words!" Crutchley said, his voice rising. "They built that palace in an hour!"

"The logic of it all is very clear, sweetie," said Korngold. "You speeded up—we saw that. The construction in the basement speeded up—you said that. The clock thing did it." She smiled. "What is there for you not to understand?"

Henry didn't answer. He'd run out of excuses. It was my turn; I couldn't go on putting it off. I had to disagree with a group of hostile adults. I had spent my whole life avoiding situations like this and had never been faced with anything nearly as bad before. I couldn't even turn and look at Henry; they'd know how frantic I was.

All I could do was pretend I was talking on the phone, making up an excuse for someone Aunt Ruth didn't want to talk to—I had done that many times. Still, my heartbeat seemed to fill the room as I said, "Oh, *I* get it. You thought what I was talking about in the basement was *real*?"

"Real? If it wasn't real, then what was it?" Crutchley burst out, his face flushing.

Yes, what was it? I wanted to hide under the table. But everything depended on me right now. I had to continue pretending I was on the phone and could hang up if it got really bad. I forced myself to continue, feeling sweat on my forehead. "That thing in the basement is . . . a set we're building for the school play. I was just practicing some of the lines. It's a science fiction play." I made an attempt at a laugh. I knew this was a really dumb story, but I couldn't think of anything else. "You don't really believe a funny toy clock could change time, do you? That's crazy. I'm really surprised that people like—"

Crutchley's face was a deep red now. He slammed both fists on the table, and the people around him recoiled, scared—and it was a physical effort for me not to cringe. He jumped to his feet. "You think you can lie your way out of this?" he shouted. "We have evidence! You saw the evidence. And there's the phone, too. We . . . we . . ." He was gasping now.

"Dad, Dad, calm down," Crutchley Junior said. "You know the doctor said it's bad for your heart to get so excited."

Crutchley put his hand to his chest. He sank back into his chair. The others all leaned toward him.

Henry grabbed my hand and pulled me to my feet. Luckily the door wasn't locked. We were out of there in seconds and running through the large room full of cubicles.

"Get them back here!" Crutchley bellowed. People in cubicles turned to look.

There were footsteps behind us now. We dashed past the receptionist, who looked vaguely up from her fingernails.

"No time to wait for the elevator," Henry said breathlessly. He ran frantically around the foyer, then found a door marked EXIT. He pushed it open, revealing a concrete stairway with a metal railing. He pulled the door gently shut behind us and we rushed down. We'd barely gone two flights before the door slammed above and footsteps started after us.

"The receptionist . . . must have told them," Henry said, gasping.

"It only sounds like . . . one person."

"Whelpley. The women probably have high heels. Crutchley and Junior—forget it. It's Whelpley. But he has a gut. We've got to beat him." He pulled at my hand, and we stopped talking and concentrated on flying down the steps.

But Whelpley was going faster than we expected. His ex-Marine footsteps seemed to be gaining on us. The exit doors had numbers on them. At the thirtieth floor, Henry put his finger to his lips and pulled me through the door.

This was not a fancy private foyer like Crutchley's. A lot of people were standing around waiting for the elevator here. We crouched behind a tall group, hoping Whelpley wouldn't know which floor we'd gotten out on.

Of course, the first elevator to chime with a down arrow was the one farthest from us. Henry barged through the crowd, pushing people out of the way—I'd never seen him like this—and we wedged into the crowded elevator just as Whelpley came pounding in from the stairway. He stood there helplessly as the elevator doors closed.

"Sorry," Henry said to the furious people glaring at us. "A crook is chasing us. We had to get away. Sorry."

"Kids today just don't have any manners; that's all I can say," a woman muttered.

There were a lot of people getting on and off; the elevator stopped at almost every floor—it was almost slower than the stairs. We squeezed to the back, but every time the door opened, we craned our necks to see if Whelpley was getting on.

"Maybe we shouldn't have run," I whispered to Henry. "Now they'll know we're scared. Now they'll know we were lying. Now they'll keep on believing it's all true."

"I know that," Henry said, sounding almost angry. "It was probably a stupid mistake to run. But I just couldn't stand to be there for one more second. They might have gotten us to admit something. And . . . and maybe that would have been worse. Right, Annie?"

"Sorry. I didn't mean to blame you. I wanted out of there, too. It probably would have been worse if we stayed."

"We haven't gotten away yet," Henry said.

At last the elevator reached the lobby. It took a long time for people to get out, and we were scanning the crowd outside. When enough people got out for us to see, there were two uniformed security guards with cellular phones, staring right at our elevator. People were still getting out of the car, blocking their view of us. But in a moment they'd see us.

I groaned. "Whelpley called them," I said. "He told them which elevator we were on. We'll never get out of here now."

"Right. We don't get out now. We go back up and get on another elevator," Henry said, pulling me to the side, behind where the buttons were, so the guards might not see us. Already other people were crowding on. In a moment we were going up.

I couldn't help smiling. "Henry, you're brilliant!"

When we got back down to the lobby, in an elevator on the other side, the guards were still watching the one we had been on before, their backs to us. We grabbed hands again and got out of the building fast.

CHAPTER THIRTEEN

We stood squeezed together in the crowded commuter train.

"What am I going to tell Aunt Ruth?"

"What am I going to tell my parents?"

Henry moved his arm to check his watch. It wasn't easy; we were really wedged in there with all the passengers. Henry had to snake his arm slowly up his side before he could get it to a place where he could read the watch. "They'll all be home by the time we get there," he said, and sighed. "Maybe it was a mistake for us to run."

"Stop blaming yourself, Henry. We both did it."

He looked at me. "You know, you were doing really fine in there," he complimented me. "I've never seen you stand up to people like that before. Good for you."

I looked away from him, blushing. But I was pleased.

It was dark and very cold on the way from the train station to my house. Still, it was a relief to be walking past soft, frosted lawns and under big old trees, instead of through the sharp concrete and glass of downtown.

"I was thinking about what you said yesterday, about how knowing about the clock keeps you out of the slow-down," Henry said. "It's the only explanation. That means if Crutchley got the clock and figured out how to make it work, they really could tear down and build things faster than anybody in the world."

All I could do was groan.

"But I still can't get over how stupid they are," Henry said, his breath steaming.

"Yeah? How are they stupid?" I wanted to hear about their stupidity; it might make me feel safer.

"Remember what Crutchley said about how they didn't need our help with the clock, they could take care of that themselves? They think they can work the clock without you and without the basement creatures. Even though on the tape you said all three elements are necessary to make a slowdown. They're not even paying attention to the evidence they stole."

"Yeah, but . . . if they think they don't need me and the

basement creatures, then that means they might just steal the clock. Then what would we do?"

Henry shrugged, hunched over, his hands in his pockets. "What if they do steal it? They can't make it work without you."

I sighed. I was scared of the clock; I didn't like it. And yet the idea of not having it in my closet bothered me in some way that I couldn't explain. "But I was never supposed to open the boxes," I told Henry. "I was never supposed to let anyone know they even existed. So if the clock gets stolen —even if they can't use it—I'll be in big trouble with Uncle Marco."

"Don't worry about that. Worry about what would happen if they *did* pay attention and *did* figure out what they really have to do to make it work."

"What do you mean?" I said, very tentatively. I didn't need anything else to worry about.

"Once they figure out they need you and the basement creatures," Henry said slowly, "then they'll *take* you and the basement creatures. They'll do something to force you to make the slowdowns they want."

"You . . . you think so?" I said miserably. But I knew he was right. Everything was just getting worse and worse. I didn't have to say that to Henry. I could tell by his manner and his tone of voice that he was scared—but not as scared as I was. Once they figured out about the clock, I would be their target.

"Oh, if only we could just forget about it for one night!" I said, clenching my fists. "But as soon as I get home, Aunt Ruth will be all over me to find out what happened."

"Yeah. My parents, too," Henry said. "We need to come up with a story to tell them. They might compare notes. And Crutchley will be in touch with them both, for sure."

We spent the rest of the way back figuring out what to say. It took a while. We had to walk slowly in the bitter cold. It was not easy coming up with a story that would satisfy all the requirements. One thing we were pretty sure of was that Crutchley wouldn't say anything to Aunt Ruth or Henry's parents about the clock. They wanted it to be a secret. It was bad enough to them that Henry and I knew.

As much as I dreaded the confrontation with Aunt Ruth, it was a relief to step into the relative warmth of the house. Of course, Aunt Ruth was too cheap to keep the furnace at anything like a comfortable level, but when you first went inside out of the cold it felt good.

She squirmed around in her chair in front of the TV as soon as she heard the door and muted the sound with the remote. "Well?" she said. "What happened? Come over here and tell me."

"Did Crutchley call you or anything?" I asked her—Henry and I agreed we had to find that out right away.

"Yeah, they did," Aunt Ruth said, eyeing me coldly as I walked around her chair and sat down on the couch, my coat still on. "They wanted to know if you were okay. They said you and the other kid ran away before they'd finished.

They want to talk to you some more." She kept staring at me. "Well? What did they want? And what stupid blunder did you two make? I promise you, Anne, if anything happens to that million-buck offer, you'll regret it—and your uncle will, too."

"They didn't tell you they were taking the offer away, did they?" I asked her hopefully.

"No, lucky for you. They hardly said anything—just that they had more to talk about with you." She glared at me balefully. "Well, Anne? *What happened?*"

Aunt Ruth thought she was such a clever bargainer, but she had just told me all I needed to know about what Crutchley had said to her. "They tried to bribe us," I said. "That's what it was all about."

"Bribe you? Why bribe *you*?" Aunt Ruth said, mystified. It wasn't the idea of bribery that bothered or puzzled her—bribery she could understand. What she couldn't understand was why they would try to bribe anybody as insignificant as Henry and me.

"I told you, I saw their spy right here at home yesterday. And they were spying on Henry's house, too. They know it's illegal to sneak into people's houses and take videos without asking. They didn't want us to tell you or anybody else."

Aunt Ruth snorted. "They didn't want you to tell *me*?"

"But it was too late—I already told you," I said. "And they didn't like that. Like I've said before, they're slimy. Henry and I couldn't take any more of it and left."

"Hmmph." Aunt Ruth was playing with her fat lower lip, one of her many irritating habits. "They didn't want me to know . . ." Aunt Ruth didn't like that, I could tell, and that was great—anything I could do to turn her against Crutchley would help. I waited for her to get angry at them.

"What did they try to bribe you with?" she asked me.

"Clothes. Trips to Disney World. Dumb things like that."

"Expensive things," Aunt Ruth pointed out. "They may be slimy, but they have money. You better call them. Here's the number they left."

I sighed. Aunt Ruth didn't care how slimy they were, as long as they were rich. And I couldn't lie and pretend to phone them. She wanted me to do it now, where she could hear, and the phone was right next to the couch.

"Oh, hello, sweetie," a woman's voice said—Danielle Korngold. "You'll have to forgive Mr. Crutchley for this afternoon. He does tend to get excited; it really isn't good for him. And sometimes it can make the wrong impression. I can understand how you two kids might have been scared away."

What was she up to? She was trying to make it sound like Adam Crutchley's temper had been the only problem this afternoon.

But that might be a good thing. It would be to our advantage if we could convince them we had been scared of his angry outburst and not scared of what they knew. "Well, Henry and I were kind of upset when he started shouting at us," I said. "We're . . . not used to that kind of thing. That's why we ran away."

"Yes, I understand, sweetie. We all do. But please don't get the wrong impression. He's a very kindhearted man—just a little excitable. We're really all just one big happy family here, really."

I wanted to gag again. The people at Crutchley were good at making me feel that way.

"So that's why we've invited both your families out to dinner tonight. At La Poulette. Of course you've heard of La Poulette; it's the best French restaurant in town. Your aunt and Henry's parents have already accepted. We'll—"

"Wait a minute," I interrupted her. "You said they already accepted?"

"Of course they did, sweetie. Who in their right mind would pass up the chance to dine at La Poulette? We'll be picking you up at seven. That should give you just enough time to get all dolled up. See you then, sweetie." And, without waiting for a response, she hung up.

I put the receiver down. Aunt Ruth's lips were pursed smugly. "Why didn't you tell me?" I asked her, angry now.

"Tell you what, Anne?" she said, as if she didn't know.

"That they invited us to dinner tonight, and you accepted."

"I figured they'd tell you themselves. Better get ready. They're coming at seven."

I didn't like this at all, and I was sure Henry didn't either.

"I don't feel like going," I said, standing up and facing Aunt Ruth squarely. "Thanks, but sorry. I've seen enough of them already today. I'm not hungry."

Aunt Ruth looked up at me, pulling on her lower lip more nervously now, not saying anything. Then she fumbled for a cigarette. What was the matter with her? She actually seemed a little frightened.

Then it hit me. This was the first time in my life I'd ever dared to resist one of her orders. A feeling of excitement rose up through my chest.

"What's . . . got into you, Anne?" Aunt Ruth said, blowing smoke in my direction. "It must be the bad influence of . . . of that other kid."

"For the tenth time, his name is Henry," I told her, waving the smoke away from my face. "Why do you refuse to remember it? And it's not his influence. I've spent enough time with Crutchley today, that's all. They take my appetite away." It was an odd feeling, speaking this way to Aunt Ruth—a feeling I liked.

Aunt Ruth just looked at me uncomfortably for a long moment. Then she thought of something. "Well, if you won't go for my sake, then go for the sake of your beloved uncle," she said, a just-perceptible certain tone in her voice. "Because if you don't go, and if you're not on your best behavior, to make up for the damage you caused this afternoon—then I cut off his annuity tomorrow. Understood?" She inhaled deeply, triumphantly.

My new confidence deserted me. She had won for now. I couldn't do that to Uncle Marco—especially not after I had betrayed him about the boxes. If only because of Uncle Marco, Aunt Ruth still had me under her thumb.

I turned and went upstairs without a word. I felt humiliated that I had given in again. I was very worried about Crutchley. Something about this dinner was wrong, really wrong. Why did they want to see all of us together, when they knew they couldn't talk about the clock or the slow-down in front of the others? What could they possibly accomplish in that situation? Were they really just trying to make up for this afternoon?

That didn't make sense. All my instincts told me not to go, to stay at home. There was something devious about their plan; I was sure of it.

But I had no choice. Aunt Ruth would be happy to cut off Uncle Marco's money.

I changed quickly—I *had* to see the basement creatures before we left for dinner. The phone rang just as I was about to go downstairs.

"Hi, Annie," Linda said. "How's it going?"

"Lousy," I told her.

She seemed a little taken aback. "Oh. Uh, well, anyway, listen. I really need to tell Jeff that—"

"Linda, I wish I could help you," I said. "But I'm completely tied up right now. I'm afraid it'll have to wait until tomorrow. I'm really sorry."

I hung up, feeling better again. I was standing up to a lot of people today, and the world hadn't ended because of it.

Aunt Ruth was still dressing. I hurried quietly down to the basement.

A sense of happy satisfaction filled my head as soon as I entered the root cellar. The creatures stood motionless in the colonnaded hallways, waiting.

One of them bowed to me from the large central archway on the ground floor, and I bowed back. *Greetings. We have been expecting you. We are very happy you did not bring the uninvited one. We are sure the Lord chastised him well.*

Now I was irritated with them, too, especially after all the trouble with Crutchley. *The "uninvited one," as you call him, is my best friend and a wonderful person and I don't know what I would do without him. And that obnoxious thing upstairs really hurt him for no reason and I'd like to tell it—*

Our minds do not accept blasphemy, it cut me off. *It is now time for you to bring the Lord down here. We are ready. We are waiting. Please do it right away.*

Huh?

We do not understand your confusion, nervous system. This is the way it is meant to be. Bring the Lord down now. The longer you wait, the greater trouble you will cause.

Now even they were making problems for me about that stupid clock! *I can't bring it down now. I have to go out. And I'll need help. I can't carry it by myself. You'll have to wait until tomorrow—I'll need the uninvited one to help me. Is that okay with you?*

We do not appreciate the hostile tone of your thinking. If you must bring another, so be it. But the longer you wait, the worse it will be—for everyone.

I'll do what I can do; that's all I can say. I've got to go now or there'll be really big trouble. I turned and crept back upstairs.

I was more bewildered than ever. Nothing was making any sense. What did the creatures mean about trouble happening if I didn't bring down the clock as soon as possible? Should I do it or not? Uncle Marco had said it was important to keep the boxes away from each other.

It was a very boring, phony, and obviously expensive dinner. Crutchley said all the purchase and sale agreements would be ready for signing the day after tomorrow, Saturday, even though he'd be in Tokyo at some big meeting by then. Whelpley wasn't there, but Korngold and Junior just kept congratulating the adults on their wise decision, and Henry and I spoke hardly a word.

We got home around ten. Aunt Ruth went right upstairs. I snuck down to the basement. The creatures were still waiting, not so patiently now. They urged me more strongly to bring the clock down to them as soon as possible. I told them again I wouldn't be able to do it until I could get Henry to help me.

But I still didn't know if I should really bring it down to

them or not. I trudged up to my room; I was wiped out and all I wanted was sleep. I opened my closet as I started to get ready for bed.

Only a fragment of a tendril lay, dry and wilted, embedded in the closet floor. The clock was gone.

I knelt on the floor and put my hands on the tendril. But it wasn't enough.

And I knew the feeling of loss wouldn't go away until I had the clock back.

CHAPTER FOURTEEN

"Crutchley stole it. That was the whole point of the dinner," Henry said at lunch the next day, Friday. "They wanted *all* of us occupied while their thieves got in."

"I knew we shouldn't have gone."

We were sitting in the cafeteria. Linda and Jeff might start asking awkward questions if we skipped lunch together three days in a row. Linda was a little cold when we sat down and asked me if I was in a better mood today. "Not really," I said. Of course, she didn't want to pursue that. And now they weren't paying any attention to us anyway.

I was really on edge, not having the clock. I picked up a French fry and put it down. I had to admit—the food at La Poulette was better than the school cafeteria. "We can't tell the police it's stolen because nobody else can know about the clock," I said. "So . . . we're on our own. What are we going to do, Henry?"

Linda and Jeff both turned and looked at me. The desperation in my voice must have been noticeable enough to intrude on their preoccupation with each other. "What's the matter, Annie?" Jeff said. "You having some kind of problem?"

I couldn't remember either of them ever asking me before about my problems; their problems were the only ones that had ever interested them. And now that they were asking, of course, I couldn't tell them.

"Nothing," I said. "Just . . ."

"You'll do fine on the math test; don't worry, Annie," Henry consoled me.

Satisfied, Linda and Jeff turned back to each other again.

"The basement creatures won't be happy," I said in an undertone. "They want the clock down there with them right away. They say that's how it's meant to be. I'm afraid to tell them it's gone."

Henry was cradling his chin in his hand, thinking. "Yeah, what are we going to do? Good question," he murmured. "Maybe . . . maybe we don't have to do anything."

"Not do anything?" I said, feeling panicky. "But what about getting the clock back?"

"Think about it," Henry said. "They'll fool around with the clock and they won't be able to get it to do anything. If we're lucky, maybe they'll bust it." He touched the sore on his cheek, which was still bright pink. "But they probably won't. They'll watch their videos again. And if they're not all total imbeciles, they'll pick up what you said about how it takes the basement creatures and you and the clock all together to make a slowdown. And then they'll come to get you—like I was saying yesterday afternoon."

"Yesterday you said they'd come and force me to make a slowdown!" I said, my voice rising again. "Do you really think—"

He quickly grimaced and put a finger to his lips. I snapped my mouth shut before anybody noticed. "We'll talk about this after school—I'll be thinking about it until then," Henry said quietly.

But after school Henry still didn't have any ideas about what to do when Crutchley came to get me.

At home, I brought him down to the basement. I didn't care that the creatures wouldn't like it. I wanted him to get their reaction to the missing clock firsthand.

It hit us both at the same time as we were approaching the root cellar—a wave of loss so bleak and so powerful we both stopped for a moment and stared at each other. They had instantly picked up the news about the missing clock.

"I'm afraid to go in there," I whispered. I understood how they felt about the clock—I missed it, too. I felt so sorry for them, I didn't know how to face them.

"Come on," Henry said.

Very quickly the fizzling impulses in our heads began to change. When we entered the root cellar, a group of the sleek ones were already dancing in the small open space in front of the palace, wearing their funny little metallic hats. Inside the palace they were dancing, too, all of them stopping frequently to bow and touch their heads to the ground. Two of the larger ones were running around the palace in opposite directions, wrapping it in the fiber that came out of their bodies.

We honor you! We honor you! We beseech you! We beseech you! We call you back to us! We call you back to us! We honor you! We honor . . .

Over and over again they repeated this chant in their heads, ignoring Henry and me completely.

Hello? Are you okay? Is there anything we can do to help? I asked them.

They paid no attention, just kept on mindlessly dancing, bowing, and chanting. There was something almost endearing—and heartrending—about the way they believed in their rituals. At the same time I was irritated that they were ignoring me; I needed their attention somehow. "Big help they are!" I whispered to Henry. We went back upstairs.

"Could you do me a favor and stay here until Aunt Ruth comes home?" I asked Henry. "I'm kind of afraid to be here alone—like if they try to kidnap me."

"You're not worried about your aunt finding me here?" Henry asked me, surprised.

"I'm tired of worrying about what Aunt Ruth thinks," I said. "She's lied to me and controlled me for my whole life —and she's gross and disgusting, too. Didn't you think so last night at dinner? You can say it."

"Well, the way we had to sit in smoking because of her —my parents were kind of appalled by that."

"Good. The worse they get along with her, the better."

"I've never heard you talk like this, Annie," Henry said, as though he wasn't sure he liked it.

I sighed. "Maybe I'm overdoing it. I don't know how to be calm and rational about fighting Aunt Ruth; I haven't had much practice. Anyway, as long as she has control of Uncle Marco's annuity, there isn't much I can do."

"Why does she have control of his annuity?" Henry asked me. "Shouldn't *he* control it?"

I had never thought of that. "I'll have to ask Uncle Marco—if I ever see him again."

"Come over to my house instead of hanging around here," Henry suggested.

I was curious about his house; I'd seen it many times, but I'd never been inside. And if Aunt Ruth didn't like me going over there with him—tough.

His house was at the top of a steep hill, slow going on the icy sidewalk. We turned off the street onto a gravel driveway, which went through a gate in a wrought-iron fence and curved slightly as it continued to climb inside their steep property. A short, bumpy lawn sloped up to the house. A couple of tall, thin cypress trees stood beside the drive, and a few other large trees took up most of the lawn.

"I didn't realize how beautiful this property was," I said, panting a little as we climbed the cracked cement steps up to the house.

"You should see it in the summer," Henry said. "Nobody gardens anymore, but there used to be a little formal garden and now it's wild, different kinds of flowers in unexpected places . . ." His voice faded. We were both thinking the same thing.

As we reached the castlelike stone building, I noticed again the crouching shape just barely visible under the dark eaves of the turret. "Is that a gargoyle up there or something?" I asked, pointing. "Why would anybody put it there? You can hardly see it."

Henry shaded his eyes against the glare of the late-afternoon winter sun. "Oh, that." He chuckled. "The shadow ghost, Dad calls it. Sometimes there's a shadow there; sometimes there isn't. Something about the light. That's why people used to joke about the house being haunted. It's nothing."

"Yeah?" I said. "Weird. I saw it on Crutchley's video, too."

The house was big but rundown. The woodwork around the windows and doors needed painting, there were missing tiles in the roof, and the small wooden outbuilding looked like it was about to collapse. Inside it was the same, with very grand, large dark rooms separated by arched double doorways. The walls were wood paneled, but the paneling needed repairs. The old wallpaper was peeling, the furniture sagged, and the Oriental rugs were threadbare.

Henry turned on a couple of lamps, which didn't do much to dispel the gloom. "If Mom and Dad had a lot of money, we could fix it up," Henry said wistfully. "But the only way they'll get a lot of money is by selling it—and then Crutchley will tear it down."

He didn't take his coat off and didn't offer to take mine. It had to be even more expensive to heat this place than to heat our house. "It's not that Mom and Dad don't love the place," Henry said apologetically. "It's just—a million dollars is a million dollars."

"I know." I sighed.

A phone rang distantly, echoing. "Hang on a minute. I'll be right back," he said, running out of the room.

I wandered over to an old built-in bookcase, but the light was almost too dim to read any of the titles. I wished the place was brighter.

Henry hurried back. "I have to go," he said. "Mom had trouble with the car and she's leaving it at the garage down on Main Street. She needs me to help her carry the groceries home."

"I better go, then," I said.

"Well, actually, if you could do us a favor, it would be

great if you stayed here. See, we only have one car." He sounded embarrassed about that. "Dad's expecting Mom to pick him up at work and she can't reach him. He'll probably phone here. It would be great if you could wait here and tell him what's going on."

I didn't feel like staying alone in this big, dark house. "Well . . . I guess so," I said.

Henry sensed my discomfort. "You'll be safer here than at your house," he said gently. "Nobody was following us. If they think you're anywhere, they'll think you're at home."

That made sense. And Henry had helped me out a lot lately. "Sure, I'll stay," I said. "When do you think you'll be back?"

"No more than half an hour," Henry said. "Thanks, Annie. Don't let Fifi out of the basement. I gotta hurry. Be sure to lock the door after I leave." We walked over to the front door. "Just turn this thing to the right."

"Okay. See you later."

Henry dashed outside and I carefully clicked on the lock and tested the door.

I was uncomfortable, but not too uncomfortable to poke around their house. What else was there to do? The kitchen was behind the stairway—and the light switch was easy to find, just inside the door. It needed remodeling more than our kitchen did. The appliances were decades old, really dated-looking. A door in the kitchen probably led to the basement, but I didn't open it to find out. I wasn't supposed to let the dog out, and I was in no mood for a dark basement anyway. The upstairs would be more interesting.

I wouldn't have gone up at all if I hadn't found the switch at the bottom of the stairs that turned on a light up above. I moved slowly, my hand on the wooden banister, boards creaking on every step. The landing had a bigger stained glass window than at our house.

The second-floor hallway was larger, too. The bedroom doors were open and I peeked into all of them, turning the light on and off in each one. Henry's room was in the front, I noticed. The only strange thing about it was a peculiar leafless vine, oddly familiar, growing out of a pot up to the ceiling on the far wall. I didn't know Henry was into plants.

The bathroom was terribly old-fashioned, with tiny white tiles and white fixtures even older-looking than the kitchen appliances and rust marks in the tub and sink. One room was a kind of study, with a big old computer, and another room was just full of junk.

The house did have more space here than a three-person family really needed. In a way it made sense for Henry's parents to sell—but not to somebody like Crutchley, who was just going to tear it down!

I kept turning around abruptly every time I heard a creak or a rustle, telling myself not to be scared. Henry had said his house made a lot of noise. I just wished it wasn't so dark. But I didn't want to leave on a lot of lights—they were probably careful about their electric bill.

I checked my watch. Only ten minutes had gone by. What was I going to do for the next twenty minutes? I could go downstairs and read a book under one of the lamps.

Or I could go up to the attic and try to get a better look at that "shadow ghost" thing. I was very curious about it. I knew I had seen it on the video at Crutchley's office. Henry said it was nothing, but I still wanted to check it out.

I turned the old-fashioned twist-switch at the bottom of the steep, narrow attic stairs, and a bleak light went on above. I climbed quickly, leaving the door below wide open—I wanted to get this over with fast. Even though I was curious, I was scared, forcing myself to go up. I also didn't want them to find me snooping around up here when they came home. The stairway turned once, and now I could see the bare bulb hanging from the beamed, sloping roof.

It was clear that Henry's family rarely if ever came up here. Cobwebs were everywhere, even on the floor; the garment bags hanging on a rack under the eaves were so heavily coated with dust I could easily have written on them with my finger.

The roofline was complicated because of the various eaves and the turret. I tried to figure out which was the front of the house—both views in which I had seen this object on the roof had been from the front. It was dark now, and all I could see outside the windows were the patches of lights from streetlamps and other houses. None of the small windows in the main attic room looked out toward a sloping lawn and the street below it.

But in one dark corner of the attic a short wooden stairway curved up to a closed door. Some of the treads were missing, so it didn't look very safe. But I thought it seemed to lead to the front of the house.

Carefully I made my way up, stepping over the black, empty places where there was nowhere to put my feet, clinging tightly to the banister with one shaky hand. How long ago had anyone come up these stairs?

At the top I turned and pushed the doorknob. At first I thought the room was locked. Then the door moved slightly but didn't open. It was stuck, warped. Obviously nobody ever came in here. I pushed harder. And suddenly, with a loud scraping noise that made me jump, the door swung open, and dust and bits of plaster fell down on me.

My heart was pounding. I couldn't find a light switch, frantically feeling on the wall just inside the door. I almost turned around and ran back downstairs.

But the moonlight and distant streetlights outside the window seemed brighter than before. I waited a minute, and my eyes began to adjust. Leaving the door wide open, I stepped inside.

From the moonlight on the round wooden ceiling I could now see that this was the top of the small, round turret. With my hands outstretched so I wouldn't bump into anything, I moved inch by inch across the floor toward the window, my heart still thudding heavily. The room smelled so stale I was sure nobody had been in here for months or even years.

My whole body was tense with fear. Why was I doing this?

Because of the boxes. Whatever the object on the roof was, I knew it couldn't be scarier than the clock—and I was so used to the clock now that I missed it.

Something brushed against my forehead and I screamed and stopped walking, my heart speeding up even more. The thing that had brushed my forehead swung back and brushed it gently again. Maybe it was nothing but a string that would turn on a light. I reached up and gave it a tug and the light came on. I moved carefully toward the window again.

There were three windowpanes, at angles to each other, a bay in the round turret. The windowsill was about the height of my chest. The ceiling light illuminated the narrow slope of the roof outside, protected by the eaves of the conical tower roof directly above.

Something sighed behind me.

I cried out and looked back toward the doorway. Nothing was there. I reminded myself again that this house just made a lot of noises.

I peered out through the glass. I could hardly see any of the roof from this angle, only a view of the sloping front lawn and the lights of the city spread below me. I'd only get a good look at what was on the roof by sticking my head out. I promised myself that if the window didn't open easily, I'd give up and hurry back downstairs.

I could see from the rusty metal latch at the top of the lower panes that the windows weren't locked. I pushed, grunting. Two of the windowpanes were immovable.

The third slid open so easily I practically fell out. Gripping the windowsill to steady myself, I craned my head outside. First I looked to the right, then to the left, sticking as much of my upper body out of the window as I safely could.

And there, to the left, almost completely hidden by the round turret roof, was the crouching figure. Finally I could see it clearly in the light from the bare ceiling bulb. A shock ran through my body; my hands tightened painfully on the windowsill.

The crouching figure was an amazingly lifelike statue of Uncle Marco.

His craggy profile was unmistakable. The statue stared out impassively over the city. It was unbelievable how lifelike Uncle Marco's long winter coat was, the bottom hem folded on the roof as the statue crouched there. I could just discern a small box next to the statue, the statue's right hand inside it. Was I dreaming this, or what?

I wasn't dreaming the headlights that suddenly careened up the driveway. I was confused. I thought Henry's mother's car was at the garage.

When the car reached the porch light, I could see that

it was long, black, and familiar—Crutchley. It stopped abruptly, wheels kicking up gravel. Two men hurried out of the vehicle. A moment later I heard footsteps downstairs.

How had they gotten in? What were they doing here?

I looked back to the statue of Uncle Marco. And as I watched, my breath coming in gasps, the statue's head very, very slowly began to move.

CHAPTER FIFTEEN

Was I going crazy or what?

Whatever was going on, I didn't want the Crutchley men to find me. I could barely stand to leave the Uncle Marco statue for even an instant, but I had no choice. I pulled off the light in the turret. Then I hurried as quietly as possible down into the main attic room, turning off a wall switch at the top of the stairs. I hoped they hadn't noticed the light from the road. Back up in the little front tower room, I quietly pulled the door shut. It scraped, but I kept pulling until it was as tightly wedged as it had been before. There was also a simple latch on it. I pushed the latch, trying to wiggle it one way, then the other. I pushed so hard the little metal pin cut painfully into my hand—and at last the pin slid home.

I checked my glowing watch dial. There were still ten minutes before Henry and his mother were due home. If only they would get back sooner!

I hurried back to the window and stretched my upper body outside again. The statue's hand inside the box moved very, very slowly. Only by staring at it could you tell it was moving at all. And the statue's head had turned farther in my direction and was no longer in profile to me.

I heard footsteps running around on the first floor, but no voices.

This was not the first time I had seen a lifelike statue moving very, very slowly. I saw the same thing watching the pedestrians during the slowdown. But there was no slowdown going on now—the Crutchley car had moved normally; the cars out on the street were moving normally; the footsteps downstairs sounded normal, too.

So if we weren't in a slowdown, what was this thing on the roof? It was gradually speeding up, the hand lifting slowly from the box, the face perceptibly turning toward me.

The footsteps now seemed to be mounting the stairs to the second floor.

It began to dawn on me, with hope, what this thing on

the roof had to be. It couldn't be a statue. It could only be Uncle Marco, for real. Uncle Marco coming out of *his own personal slowdown.*

I didn't know why he had put himself into a slowdown or why he had chosen to do it on Henry's roof. Neither fact made any sense. But they were facts: This was Uncle Marco—who could maybe help me escape from the Crutchley henchmen running through the house, if he could get unfrozen fast enough.

The kidnapping I was avoiding by not being at home was happening to me here.

Uncle Marco's head was now three-quarters turned. I stretched farther out over the roof so that maybe he could see me. I stuck out my hand and waved it frantically. "Uncle Marco!" I said. "Uncle Marco! It's me, Annie!"

Then I remembered with a horrible pang: Uncle Marco had forbidden me to open the boxes. I was in this mess because I had disobeyed him. I had never disobeyed him before. He had every reason to be angry at me—very, very angry. Maybe it would be better if he didn't find me here.

But what choice did I have? It was either Uncle Marco or the men from Crutchley.

"Uncle Marco!" I said again, speaking loudly out in the cold winter air where the men wouldn't hear on the floors below. "Can't you hear me?"

Then I realized what I was doing wrong. I was talking too fast. He was only gradually coming out of stasis. To him, I would be a blur, and my voice would be high-pitched, unintelligible babble.

"Uncle . . . Marco," I said very, very slowly and deeply, stretching out all the consonants. I sounded like a ghostly voice in a bad horror movie, and I felt foolish, but I kept on going, pitching my voice as low as possible. "It's . . . me . . . Annie. . . . Can . . . you . . . hear . . . me?"

His head still wasn't facing me directly—he couldn't move that fast yet. Gradually the mouth began to open. Then a voice came out, deeper, more spectral and creepy than mine. "Youououooah," Uncle Marco groaned.

My mind, full of guilt, was rushing crazily. Was he saying "You"? Was he accusing me of something—like opening the boxes and making a slowdown?

The footsteps ran from room to room on the floor below.

Could Uncle Marco know about the slowdown? Was that why he was coming out of this? I tried to think rationally.

If Uncle Marco was in his own slowdown, the rest of the world would be a speedy blur to him—under normal conditions. Then, last Tuesday, he would easily have noticed that everything was going a lot slower.

But if he was coming out of this because of the slowdown, then why had he waited three days?

"Oh, Uncle Marco, you don't know just how sorry—" I started to say in a normal voice. I caught myself. He wouldn't be able to hear that. I started again. "I'm . . . sorry . . . about . . . slowdown." I made myself pause for a long time so the meaning would sink in. "Why . . . you . . . wait . . . three . . . days?"

He had turned his head enough so that our eyes finally met—his wonderful ice blue eyes, now so slow-moving. His mouth was thawing; his voice was a little faster and higher-pitched now. "Didn't . . . wait. . . . Takes . . . time."

He must have been *incredibly* slowed down if it took him three whole days to come out of the stasis. I realized then that the box next to him had to be his personal clock. He seemed to have the ability to work it on his own, without needing any basement creatures the way I did.

The footsteps were now pounding loudly on the attic stairs. How long would it take them to find us?

Uncle Marco was speeding up more quickly now. His hand was completely out of the box, and his head was facing me directly. Like a slow-moving night creature, he oozed smoothly toward the window on his hands and knees, his coat dragging, crawling over the box, leaving it there on the roof. I moved my body back into the room. He crouched on the roof facing the window. "Caaaaarrrrr?" he asked me in that deep voice.

"Crutchley Development," I said, not as slowly now. And Uncle Marco—his head stretched forward, poised and listening hard—was close enough that I could speak softly and hope not to be heard by the men clomping around in the attic. "They found out about the slowdown. They want to do it themselves, for fast construction. They stole the clock. They offered a million for our house and this one. Aunt Ruth and these people will sell."

He was moving fast enough now so that I could see his face twist into a grimace of pain. He shook his head. "Can't sell. Can never sell," he said, sounding like the Frankenstein monster.

"They're here to take me. They figured out they need me to make a slowdown for them—they want me to show them how to do it." I grabbed his hand, on the windowsill now. It was cold as ice. "Help me, Uncle Marco! What can we do?"

His face melted back to normal. He was thinking, staring at me. Was he furious? Was there anything we could do to stop Crutchley? And it was all my fault!

"I'm sorry, Uncle Marco!" I whispered. "You don't know how sorry I—"

"Go with them," he said, without expression, his voice at almost normal speed now. "Go with them and make a slow-down."

"Huh?" That was the last thing in the world I expected to hear.

"Ask the clock to make the deepest, longest slowdown possible. Go with them. Do it. Don't let them in here."

"But that's . . . that's *crazy*, Uncle Marco! You don't understand! If they can make a slowdown, then they can—"

"Do it." There was still no expression on his face or in his voice. He must really be furious! "Do it! Make a slowdown. Don't let them in."

He turned and crawled away from the window.

"But . . ."

"Do it!" Uncle Marco said and moved out of sight.

He wasn't going to save me. He wasn't even going to help me! He was sending me off to Crutchley on my own, to do exactly what they wanted me to do. He must be more furious at me than I could even imagine. Was he punishing me? Was he giving up? I didn't understand.

Then I remembered he had said, "Can't sell. Can never sell." That must mean he wasn't giving up.

But then why did he want me to show Crutchley how to make a slowdown? It was incomprehensible.

But Uncle Marco was telling me to do it. He was very clear. And that meant I had no choice. I had to go to Crutchley by myself. He was saying, "You got us into this mess on your own. Now you get us out on your own."

The door began to shake. They were banging on it. "Hellooo! We're here to help!" a man shouted outside the door.

I pulled the window shut. I turned. Suddenly, because of the unreality of everything, I was more numb than frightened. I looked at my watch. Henry and his mother should have been back before now. What had happened to them?

I had to do what Uncle Marco told me, even though it went against common sense. Following his orders now was the only way to make up for the trouble I had caused by disobeying him before.

And he didn't want them coming into this room.

"Wait," I called out. "I'll be right out." I unlatched the door and pulled it open.

CHAPTER SIXTEEN

The two men hovered around me.

"Lucky we found you!"

"You okay? They were worried about you."

They were wonderful liars, these young men from Crutchley in their dark suits.

They peered over my shoulder into the tower room. Uncle Marco didn't want them in there. If they went in, they might see him—and his box—on the roof. "Who were you talking to?" they asked me.

"I talk to myself when I'm scared." I shut the door behind me.

"We better check out that room."

"I'm going now." I pushed past them down the curving flight of stairs into the main attic, walking fast. They stayed with me, leaving the door to the tower room closed.

"Are you taking me to the office, or what?" I said on the way downstairs. I had the same feeling now as I had when standing up to Aunt Ruth yesterday—I didn't care how they would react, and it felt good. Sure, I was scared. But I wasn't scared of these guys. They were just underlings. I knew I was smarter than they were.

"Mr. Crutchley and them are real concerned. They just need to talk to you to be sure everything's okay."

Everything *was* going okay now—for them.

"Take me home first, please," I said. "You know how close it is. I can't do what they want unless I bring something from my house."

"Sorry. Our orders are—"

But I knew they had to be careful with me; if they used force, it could kill the deal. I stopped on the stairs and crossed my arms. "Then I'm not going without a fight. It'll slow things down. Henry and his parents might get back. If you'll let me talk to somebody at the office—any one of those people—they'll tell you to let me stop off at home first."

They didn't like it, but one of them got out a cellular phone. Korngold answered. "Oh, hello, sweetie!" she gushed. "We're so relieved to hear your voice. We were so worried when you didn't get home and—"

"I can't do what you want unless I get some of the creatures from my basement," I said to her. "I have to have them and the clock or it won't work. Do you remember that from your tape? Play it again if you don't believe me. Then tell these guys to let me stop at home for five minutes."

She told them.

"One of you come in with me and be polite to Aunt Ruth," I said in the car. "That way she'll think what you're doing is legit."

They looked at each other. They clearly hadn't been expecting me to behave like this. "Who says this isn't legit?" one of them asked me. "We're just helping to—"

"Whatever," I interrupted. "It'll be faster and easier if one of you comes in with me."

Aunt Ruth was just switching on the TV. She turned when she heard the door open and said automatically, "Anne, you ungrateful brat! Where have you been? You're not allowed to just disappear without—"

Then she saw the man from Crutchley and her mouth snapped shut.

"Uh, evening," he said. "We just gotta take her to the office—Crutchley Development. They have to talk a little more—then you'll be able to close the deal."

"Huh? What?" Aunt Ruth said, not pleased. "Why do they need to talk to her so much? Why aren't you telling me what's going on?"

"I'll be back in a minute. You two can entertain each other," I said.

The creatures in the basement were still going at their ritual, though I could now detect a weariness and hopelessness in the impulses I was getting. *I'm going to see the Lord now,* I thought, hoping they would listen.

The chanting went on.

I'm going to the Lord! I projected more intensely. *The Lord needs your help now!*

The dancing stopped. There was a confused babble. Their heads swung back and forth. Finally one of the sleek ones stepped forward and bowed. I bowed back.

You say you are going to the Lord? But that is not your duty now, nervous system. Your duty is to bring the Lord here.

It was so obstinate I wanted to kick it. But at least it was straightforward—which was a lot better than most of the human beings I was dealing with. *I am not in control of the situation. Others, more powerful than I am, have stolen the Lord. But now they will take me to It. If you want to communicate with It—and make a sacrifice—this is your only chance. I must make a slowdown now. I need your help. It is the only way to get the Lord back here.*

This request was so unusual that I had to spell it out several times before it began to sink in. Then they conferred with each other. And finally, once again, four creatures from the top level were chosen by battle and presented themselves to me. I found a small cardboard carton and put them inside it and rushed upstairs.

I had sworn I would never do this again. But I sensed that the creatures—and the clock—wanted it. And I was part of them now.

Aunt Ruth and the driver had given up trying to talk to each other. He was tapping his foot and she was glowering. I was sure he didn't know what they really wanted with me—the slowdown had to be top secret. He turned and looked at me with great relief when I came in.

"Let's go," I said.

"Anne! *What is going on?*" Aunt Ruth demanded furiously.

"They want to talk to me. I'll tell you all about it when I come back." I hurried out the door.

It was 5:45. We drove against traffic on the highway—the lanes going out of town were full, and ours was almost empty. Wind rattled against the car. Clouds had quickly covered the moon; it was beginning to snow. We got to their offices more quickly than I wanted. And even though it was after five, the big purple-and-silver room was full of Crutchley wage slaves crouched over terminals in their cubicles—there was no way they could even tell it was snowing outside.

We didn't go to the fancy conference room this time. We went past that door, through another door that had to have a security code punched into a small device on it. Whelpley, who had not been at dinner last night, was waiting on the other side of the door in a small, unadorned cement anteroom. He didn't smile or wink at me this time; his expression was stony. Henry and I had successfully eluded him the day before, and he didn't like that.

"Good evening," was all he said. He nodded at the driver, who left me there and went back through the same door we had entered. Where we were going must be too high security for him.

The next door was metal, a double door, with a curved, U-shaped metal handle on each side. It required another, longer security code. Whelpley pressed buttons for a while, then pulled the door open and waved me through.

This room was bigger than the conference room. The floor space was taken up by two trestle tables, and drafting equipment, and blueprints on big easels. Several mainframe computer terminals reposed on large metal desks, and rows of filing cabinets lined the walls, as well as lots of shelves and cubbyholes. The secretary, Ms. MacElberg, sat at another desk typing on a typewriter. Through two normal-sized windows on one wall, you could see the lights of the city and the wind wildly whipping the snowflakes around.

Crutchley was standing at the head of one of the tables. Korngold and Junior rose to their feet. The clock sat, heavy and silent, on the table in front of them. I wanted to run over and touch it.

Beside the table was an industrial dolly, a low metal cart with four big wheels. That was what they must have used to get the box in here.

Crutchley smiled at me and came over and squeezed my shoulder. "Well, young lady, I'm glad you've made the right decision," he complimented me. "You made no problems on the way over here, and you insisted on bringing what you needed from home. We checked the tape, like you said. Good for you!" He rubbed his hands together, his grin widening. "Now let's get to work and see exactly how to make this thing do what we want." He looked at his watch. "I'm catching a flight to Tokyo tonight and if I want to make the right kind of scheduling bids, I'll need to know—" He paused, still smiling. "Well, I won't bore you with all that."

He wasn't even trying to hide his excitement. The others, I now realized, were tense with anticipation, too. And why shouldn't they be? Once Crutchley had the ability to slow down the rest of the world, they'd be the richest development company *in* the world.

And I was about to show them how to do it.

Why had Uncle Marco told me to do this? I couldn't figure it out. But he had said it in so many words.

I walked toward the table with the metal box on it, the numbness gone now, replaced by a miserable, sick churning in my stomach. Maybe I wouldn't be able to do it because I was going to throw up. But that would be only a short delay. I was locked in here with them and with everything necessary. There was no way out anymore.

I approached the clock. They hadn't busted it; it looked exactly the same, sinister and implacable and necessary to me now. I bowed, with real feeling. *We need another slowdown. The deepest, longest slowdown you can possibly make.*

I set the cardboard carton on the table, opened it, and took out the four creatures, which scrabbled around on my hands. Korngold put her hand to her mouth and took a step back. Junior gulped, looking pale. Whelpley and Crutchley leaned forward, fascinated.

I had told the creatures this was the only way to get the clock back where they wanted it. Like before, they staunchly waited on each of the four propellers.

The clock clicked once. The tendrils didn't move.

We were all bending over it now. "Well? Why isn't anything happening?" Crutchley said impatiently.

I remembered what the clock had done to Henry. "You have to think at it, ask it to make a slowdown. It can't be rushed," I said. And I thought, *Please. The deepest slowdown you can make. And a long one, too. It's the only way we can get you back home with the basement creatures, where they say you belong.*

A tendril shot out and grabbed Crutchley's cheek. Korngold shrieked, the men shouted, Crutchley wailed. Whelpley grabbed the tendril, trying to pull it away.

Right on! I thought.

They managed to get the tendril away from Crutchley, who was now whimpering, "Oh, oh, oh!" with his hand on his face.

"Did you make it do that?" Whelpley accused me.

Maybe I had; I had imagined it, and the clock might have been doing my bidding. "I'm just doing the same thing I did last time; that's all I know," I told him. "And last time it started after I—"

"Wait! Look! Something's happening!" Korngold cried.

We all bent over it again, even Crutchley. It was clicking like crazy, the propellers moving. Four tendrils, all at once, reached out and crushed the poor little creatures—it wasn't taking its time like before. The propellers moved faster and faster.

I turned to the window. The car lights on the streets and bridges stopped abruptly, not gradually like last time; snow stabilized in midair. "Look!" I said, scared but also excited at what was happening in spite of myself. "Look out there and watch the world stop!"

There was no answer. I turned back.

Crutchley and the others didn't seem to have heard me. They were all bent over the clock, staring down at it without moving.

Frozen.

"Hey," I said. "Can't you . . . Don't you . . ."

And then—finally—it hit me.

I whooped with joy. I backed away from them. And then I was dancing around the room, clapping my hands.

Of course this was the right thing to do—why had I ever doubted Uncle Marco? And why hadn't I realized this before?

I was the nervous system, the only one who could make the clock work. And whenever I did make a slowdown, *Crutchley and Company would be caught in it, too.* And so would all their machinery and all their workmen. Knowing about the clock didn't keep you out of the slowdown. Crutchley would never be able to use the clock, no matter what. We were safe from that. We had always been safe. We just hadn't been smart enough to know it.

And now, here I was in the middle of the deepest, longest slowdown yet—in the frozen inner sanctum of Crutchley Development. I was in the perfect position to run around and carefully disable them; all their computers, all their files, all their blueprints were right here for me to go through and cleverly tamper with. This was my chance to put them out of business forever and save our neighborhood.

And I had no idea what to do.

I screamed in frustration.

"Calm down. Wait a minute," I said out loud. "You're not alone." And I wasn't. Henry and Uncle Marco would not be trapped in the slowdown either—Henry because he hadn't been last time, for some reason I still didn't understand, and

Uncle Marco because he had his own clock. Henry and Uncle Marco were smart. They would both know exactly what to do to disable Crutchley Development.

And Henry and Uncle Marco were both twenty miles away, in the suburbs. Every conveyance between there and here, every car, every taxi, every train, was frozen, trapped in the slowdown.

CHAPTER SEVENTEEN

I was on my own.

I looked around, trying to think through my panic. Computers, files, blueprints. Where should I begin?

I didn't have a computer at home; Aunt Ruth thought they were an expensive luxury. I often worked on the computers at school, but I knew how to use only those particular simple programs. I had no idea how to get into a mainframe and look for secret data. Henry might be able to do it, but Henry wasn't here.

I screamed again and stamped my foot. This was probably our only chance to get Crutchley and save our houses. What was I going to do?

I ran over to the filing cabinets. I found the *L* file. At first the drawer didn't want to budge. I gave it a really hard yank and it rolled slowly toward me. I pawed through the sluggish, heavy papers as quickly as I could, my hands shaking, looking for our last name, Levi. There was a folder with our name on it; I tugged it open. It contained letters that Crutchley had written to us in the past, old offers that Aunt Ruth had rejected. There was also a kind of resumé about Aunt Ruth and a very short one about me. There was nothing about Uncle Marco. I knew it was his intention that people know as little about him as possible. He had succeeded.

But there was nothing illegal here, nothing damaging to Crutchley.

It took a lot of effort to get the file drawer moving, but once started, it crept forward with inevitability and finally clanged shut with a long, brittle sound like a drumroll, which echoed eerily in the large room.

I turned around, wondering where else to look. It was odd to see the four people bending over the spinning propellers of the clock and behind them the nearly motionless lights and snowflakes outside the window. The people weren't actually statues—Crutchley's eyeballs were moving slightly toward the window and Whelpley was gradually turning his head—but they were slow enough so that they couldn't interfere with me. The clock and I were the only things that moved normally, my breathing and the clock's whirring the only faint sounds in the silent, frozen world.

Then I noticed the secretary, seated at a desk with a typewriter on it on the other side of the room; she wasn't facing the typewriter; she had turned her chair around to look at the clock at the moment she froze. If that was her normal workstation, there might be some more recent papers there that could be useful. I hurried over.

And on the desk where she had been working was a pile of about two dozen very legal-looking documents: STANDARD FORM PURCHASE AND SALE AGREEMENT, the top one said in big letters. I thumbed through the pile. They were all purchase and sale agreements.

I looked through them again, more carefully. The buyer in every case was Crutchley Development Corporation, represented by Adam Crutchley. The sellers were all different, and many of the names were familiar to me. The addresses of the properties were all in our neighborhood.

These were the documents that would finalize Crutchley's buying out our neighborhood so that he could tear down the houses and turn it into a giant mall. He had said they'd be ready tomorrow.

My first impulse was to destroy them. I lifted the top one to tear it to shreds.

I stopped myself in time. If I destroyed them, all they'd have to do was make new ones when the slowdown was over. Tearing them up wouldn't stop Crutchley.

But I still had the feeling there might be something useful here. I looked the documents over more carefully. They were all signed by Crutchley, but not by the sellers. That was interesting—and it seemed a little foolish.

But he was about to leave for Tokyo, and they were in a hurry to finalize these purchases. With his signature on the agreements, his staff could close the deals while he was gone. After all, the forms were perfectly safe here, locked away behind two security doors that only his closest cohorts could get through. No one would ever expect that someone—like me—could get in here and get her hands on them.

The buyers hadn't signed them yet. The space for the date was still blank. Was there anything else that had been left out? I checked through them one more time, more slowly and carefully than ever.

Clause number seven, PURCHASE PRICE, also had a blank spot that had not yet been typed in on about half the forms. I blinked, and shook my head, and checked again. The empty space was in front of a line labeled "are to be paid at the time of the delivery of the deed, in cash, or by certified cashier's, treasurer's, or bank check."

The amount to be inserted there must be the final purchase price that Crutchley had to pay. Where it was typed in, the prices were mostly between $70,000 and $100,000. Why hadn't the others been typed in yet? Probably because they were still doing the last-minute final negotiations, trying to get the sellers to settle for as low a price as possible.

As low a price as possible . . .

That gave me an idea. My heart began to pound. Would this really work?

I set the purchase and sale agreements down carefully and turned to Ms. MacElberg's typewriter. She had been typing in the blanks on one more purchase and sale agreement when I had come into the room. That meant this was the typewriter that had the legal clout for these documents.

The idea I was beginning to come up with was crazy and so wonderful I hardly dared to believe I could get away with it. I wasn't a legal expert, and maybe Crutchley would find a way around this. But what was there to stop me from trying? I couldn't think of anything else to do.

I was also aware that the slowdown could stop at any instant. It had already gone on longer than the last one. And I couldn't depend on the clock to help me out and extend it for as long as I needed—it was nasty and unreliable.

Still, I ran over and bowed to it. *Please, please, keep this one going as long as you possibly can. Remember, we're connected. It's the only way you'll ever get back to your worshipers in the basement.*

Back at the typewriter, I was trembling more than before, my heart still thudding. Ms. MacElberg was in the way, of course, in her secretary's chair on wheels. With great effort, I tried to push her chair so I could have access to the typewriter keyboard. At first the chair didn't want to move.

Panting, I pushed and pushed, and finally it began to roll. It rolled several feet, rocking slowly over bumps in the linoleum floor, Ms. MacElberg with her bun and glasses swaying stiffly on the seat. Finally it slowed and stopped.

I approached the keyboard nervously. Ms. MacElberg hadn't made any mistakes, and I couldn't either. The power light on the typewriter was flickering green. Under normal conditions the machine would have been humming. Now it was making very infrequent, long, drawn-out thumps—very distant and faint in the deep, deep quiet of the room.

The first thing I wanted to type in was the date—the space for this was at the very top of the document, and the paper was now about halfway down into the typewriter. I had to move it back up to the top.

I carefully pushed down on the key with the up arrow. Like the telephone keys during the last slowdown, it didn't want to move. I had to put more pressure on it than I expected. Finally, with a kind of sigh, the key sank down. I held it there. The carriage trembled and very slowly moved, and the paper went down one notch. Then another notch. Then another. I lifted my finger when the blank space for the date seemed to be in the right place.

Today was the fifteenth; I would put in today's date so the sellers would sign immediately. I patiently depressed the 1 key. When I finally got it all the way down, the metal ball inside the typewriter went into action. Normally these things flashed so fast you couldn't see them. Now it glided centimeter by centimeter toward the document, turning languidly as it went. Finally it made contact with the paper like a long, lingering kiss and began its leisurely journey back into the typewriter again. It took a long time, but I was pleased—the number was in just the right spot on the page.

When at last the date was finished, I moved the paper back down to the space for the purchase price. How much? I pondered. I didn't want to make it too unrealistic. On the other hand, I might not have enough time to do all the empty purchase and sale agreements. I had to make sure the ones I did do were enough.

I went to work. After what felt like fifteen minutes, I had typed in a purchase price of 100 million dollars.

I hadn't even noticed whose house this was. I glanced up at the seller's name. "Nathan and Elizabeth Vail," it said. I smiled. I figured Henry wouldn't have much trouble getting his parents to sign this.

I put it down quickly. At any moment time could start up again and I'd have to run out of here. But there was no way I could go any faster—the typewriter physically couldn't do it. I went on working, my hands moist now, the tension in my body constant and grinding. I kept praying for the clock to please just give me enough time to do another one. I turned back often to check on the people. They were all looking toward the window now.

At the back of my mind, in the deep silence, I was also worrying about keeping my promise to the clock and the creatures. I had to get it home, for me and the creatures. But how?

I was on the fifth 100-million-dollar purchase and sale agreement when the banging began.

I jumped about a foot into the air. Now my heart was pounding more wildly than ever.

The banging outside the room—not on the door to this room, but not very far away—continued.

The sound was unnatural, impossible—the world was frozen. What did it mean? Henry and Uncle Marco wouldn't have been able to get here this fast. Who else could be outside the slowdown?

I forced myself to finish the agreement, my hand shaking more than ever; got it out of the typewriter; and started for the door. Then, just to be safe, I picked up the five finished agreements and took them with me.

The banging went on, unabated. Whoever was making it was very determined to get in—and seemed to believe that there was somebody inside who could hear it. Who would believe that in the middle of this arctic slowdown? I hesitated. Maybe it would be better to ignore the noise and let whoever was making it give up and go away.

But I was too curious.

I had to push very, very hard to get the door out of this room to begin to move. When it did, it moved slowly enough for me to think and remember not to stupidly lock myself out—I didn't know the security code. I took off my shoe and stuck it in the door so it wouldn't close.

The banging was coming from the next door, the first one with a security device on it. I crossed the cement anteroom. Holding my breath, I looked through the little glass peephole in the door.

"Henry!" I shouted and pushed open the door.

Henry tumbled inside, gasping for breath. We hugged each other awkwardly. "C-Crutchley?" he wheezed, his chin on my shoulder.

"They're all frozen. Like everybody else. We should have known. It was so great when it happened!"

"Oh, wow!" was all he could say.

"How did you get here? How did you know I was here?" I asked him, pulling away.

He slumped against the wall, panting, too breathless to speak.

"Come on. We'll talk in here. I've got work to do," I told him. I pulled the double door open with one of the two U-shaped handles, picked up my shoe and slipped it on, and we went inside.

I was already typing the next document by the time Henry had looked around the room and caught his breath enough to talk.

"So . . . we still don't know why I don't freeze like everybody else," he said.

"Nope," I said, pushing down on a key and watching the ball perform its slow adagio over to the paper and come moping back. "They're not really frozen," I said. "They've all turned toward the window since it started."

"What are you doing?" he wanted to know.

I smiled. "Look at this," I said, handing him the purchase and sale agreement for his house. "Didn't I do a good job? He'd already signed it but left off the date and purchase price. I put them in. I'm on my sixth one now."

Henry looked at it curiously. Then his head shot forward; his eyes widened; he turned to me. "Uh . . . a hundred million?" he murmured.

"This one's mine," I said. "*We're* getting two hundred million."

Henry burst into laughter. He was laughing so hard he couldn't stand up. He sank down onto the floor, rolling in mirth, clutching his sides. Now I was laughing, too.

Finally Henry wiped his eyes and was able to say, "This will kill him! These signed forms mean he's legally obliged to pay all this money. He won't be able to. He'll have to go out of business, bankrupt!"

"You got it." I finished the one for our house. "Let me have another one."

He hugged me again, quickly. "Annie, you're a genius!" he said and handed me another agreement.

"I'm not a genius." I worked the paper into the typewriter. "Crutchley's just an idiot. Oh! I forgot to tell you. I found the shadow ghost on your roof. It was Uncle Marco."

Henry peered at me. "What are you talking about?"

"Uncle Marco was in his own slowdown on your roof, with his own clock. Don't ask me why. He was just coming out of it. He told me to come here and make a slowdown. If he hadn't told me, I might have resisted more or maybe not even done it. Lucky thing I found him."

Henry was shaking his head. "I still don't understand why he would . . ."

"Neither do I. How did you get here so fast?"

"I called the house from the garage to tell you we were going to be late. You weren't there." I looked over at him. He wiped sweat off his forehead, then shrugged off his coat onto the floor. "I knew Crutchley got you—and was going to force you to make a slowdown. I told Mom I had to go and got a taxi for downtown right away. Every second I was afraid the slowdown was going to start and I'd get stuck before I got here. We were just coming off the highway when it happened. I had to get out of the cab and find my way here—and then climb thirty-nine flights." He slouched against the desk.

"How did you know which doorway to knock on?" I asked him, starting to type in another 100 million.

"Nobody was in the conference room. Then I saw the door with the security lock on it. I figured that's where they'd take you. I just kept banging away." He looked at the five people in the room, grinning. They were turning away from the window toward us now. "Why didn't we realize this is what would happen to them? What a relief! I was so worried about you." Then his smile faded. "Uh-oh," he said.

"Huh?" I was concentrating on finishing the form.

"We're in trouble."

"What? What's the matter?"

"Look. Out the window."

I turned impatiently.

The snowflakes were just beginning to slide past the glass.

CHAPTER EIGHTEEN

"We gotta get out of here!" I said, pushing the arrow key to move the form out of the typewriter. "If they catch us, it'll ruin everything."

Henry bent over and grabbed his coat. "Come on, let's go!" he said, heading for the door.

The form was still click-clacking its way out of the typewriter. "But . . . we have to bring the clock."

"What?" Henry turned back, frowning. "How? Why?"

At last the form worked its way out; I set it on top of the others. The snowflakes were still barely moving. I remembered how slowly Uncle Marco had come out of his stasis. "Because I promised it and the creatures. Anyway, I don't want to leave it here."

"But . . ." Henry shook his head. "We can't risk them getting those forms!"

Normally I wouldn't have been so pushy. But I didn't think I could physically leave the room without the clock. I also couldn't let the creatures down; they were depending on me. "If we can get the box on the dolly, it won't take long. Come on!"

We rushed over to the table. The four figures were moving faster now, still turning toward the back of the room, where I'd been typing. The propeller was gradually slowing down, now that time was starting up again.

I put the papers down on the table, and Henry and I began trying to push the clock toward the edge. It was difficult to get things to move, just coming out of a slowdown, and the clock was heavy under normal conditions. We were both grunting as we inched it across the table —lucky for us that the four melting statues were all at one end and not in the way.

At last we got it to the edge. I looked away for a moment. The four people were turning toward us now, away from the back of the room—maybe we were no longer a blur to them.

Henry and I were each gripping two bottom corners of the metal box. "One. Two. *Three!*" Henry said.

We lifted it and staggered, both groaning, and dropped it with a crash onto the dolly.

One of Crutchley's hands began to lift from the table.

"Come on!" Henry said, grabbing the handle of the dolly. I pushed from behind. We headed for the door. We had almost reached it when Henry turned back. *"The agreements!"* he screamed.

I rushed back to the table, my entire body ringing with panic. I carefully picked up the six forms, not wanting to tear them. Crutchley was beginning to reach out with one hand. Whelpley's eyes were right on me. Korngold's red-lipsticked mouth was opening. In a minute they'd be able to chase us. I dashed for the door.

Henry had rushed back into the room, too. Now he was exiting through the double doors with a long metal ruler from one of the drafting tables. I started through myself, about to ask him what he was doing.

At the same time my mind was racing ahead, thinking about exactly what we were going to do with the forms. "Keep going, Henry!" I said, and ran back into the room, over to the secretary's desk. She was beginning to move her chair back toward the desk. I looked through various piles and cubbyholes. "Whaaaaaa?" I heard Whelpley saying behind me.

At last I found what I wanted. I grabbed some envelopes and raced back to the door and paused only a second to look back and see Whelpley's eyes on me now. He took a step in my direction; he was coming out of it faster than the others.

I pushed through the door. Henry was standing there with the ruler. "Hurry! They're moving faster!" I told him.

"You're the one who said we had to bring the clock!" Henry said, so frantic his voice was high-pitched. "And then you ran back again. We've got to slow them down." He smashed the security panel with the ruler. "That'll jam the lock," he said. "And just to make extra sure . . ." He stuck the heavy metal ruler through the two U-shaped handles on the double doors. "Now they're stuck in there," he said, and pulled the dolly through the next door.

The people in the big silver-and-purple office were shifting within their cubicles; lights fluttered slowly on monitors. We trundled the dolly past them, past the receptionist, to the elevators. Henry pushed the button. Eventually the elevator call light blinked on.

"If we don't get an elevator right away, we're leaving this here!" he said furiously.

"Why are you so mad at me?" I shouted at him, gripping the purchase and sale agreements.

"Because you had it all worked out perfectly and you're going to ruin it by trying to bring this stupid thing. Come on, please, let's just take the stairs!"

"Another minute. Thirty seconds!" I pleaded.

Sounds were awakening now, rustlings, breathings, slow footsteps. Henry and I were both madly pacing past the elevators.

I bent over the clock. *Slow it down, can't you? We're taking this big risk for your sake!* I pleaded with it. But the propeller's speed continued to slacken.

"What . . . are . . . you . . . doing . . . here?" a deep voice asked.

We turned. The receptionist was thawing fast. She blinked a couple of times. When we didn't answer, she said, "Where . . . did . . . you . . . come . . . from?"

"Forget this thing and take the stairs!" Henry hissed. "They'll be here in a second."

But I wouldn't forget the clock. I had never been so stubborn.

At that moment a sound like a low-pitched xylophone reverberated through the elevator bank. Green light poured into the Down arrow across from us. We rushed over. As the doors opened very, very slowly, we heard the footsteps.

"Don't look! Just get in!"

We dragged the dolly into the elevator and Henry pushed 1 and then CLOSE. We waited.

I peeked outside. The driver in the dark suit was approaching, speeding up.

The doors began to close. Henry was bent over, his fists clenched. "Hurry! Hurry! Hurry!" he was praying under his breath.

The driver lumbered toward us at almost a normal pace, though from his red face and the way he was leaping between strides I could tell he was trying to run. He reached out to push the elevator button and stop us.

The doors closed. A moment later the elevator was sinking.

"Oh, we made it!" I sighed, sliding back against one wall.

Then I panicked again. The elevator fell faster and faster.

Henry and I gripped each other and I dropped the forms. "It's falling!" I screamed.

"I don't think so," Henry said, but he didn't sound too sure. "It might just be picking up speed because the slow-down's stopping."

The elevator slowed gradually just as we reached the lobby. I quickly gathered up the forms from the floor. The chime sounded perfectly normal as the doors opened. We pulled the dolly into the lobby, full of people on their way home from work. I tucked the purchase and sale agreements and envelopes carefully under my coat. Henry dragged the dolly out of the building into the swiftly falling snow and over to the curb and waved for a taxi.

"If we don't get one in one minute, we're leaving this thing here and taking the train," Henry threatened. We kept looking back desperately toward the building. Several empty taxis passed us by.

"It's because we're teenagers," Henry said bitterly. "If we were adults, one of them would have stopped already."

I rushed out as the next taxi passed and waved frantically. And it stopped. The Crutchley team wasn't coming out of the building as we maneuvered the clock inside—they must still be trapped in that room. Henry started to give the driver my address.

"No," I said. "We'll be making a lot of stops in that neighborhood." I looked through the purchase and sale agreements. "Better go to One Thirty-nine Brookdale Avenue first."

One by one I carefully folded the forms and put them into the printed Crutchley Development envelopes. "You got a pen, Henry?" I asked him when we were on the highway.

He handed it over to me. "What are you doing?"

"Making sure they sign right away." The moving car would make my hand unsteady, but I didn't think it mattered. I wasn't going to try to imitate anybody's handwriting—once the sellers saw what was inside, they wouldn't notice. "Congrats, sweetie!" I wrote on the envelope. "Please sign right away. Danielle."

When we got to our neighborhood, the driver stopped at the first house and I ran out and slipped the envelope through the mail slot on their door. Back inside the taxi, I said, "Okay. Now go to—"

"Wait a minute," the driver said doubtfully. "How many houses we stopping at?"

I looked at the meter, which was on twenty-five dollars now. "Just do what we say and you'll get a minimum of fifty," I told the driver.

I dropped off six agreements, including Henry's—he stayed in the taxi so he could help me carry the clock into my house. "Okay, we can go home now," I said and gave the driver my address.

The meter was on forty dollars when we got there. Henry

and I looked at each other. Neither of us had the money. But I wasn't worried; I was exhilarated. "Wait here. I'll be right out with the money," I said.

Aunt Ruth was *still* in front of the TV. Again, she turned with automatic anger at the sound of the door. "Home so soon? You'll be happy to know that man is back again. The deadbeat wasn't even gone a week. I can't wait for you to tell him I'm going to kill his annuity and—"

I'd already reached her chair. "May I have fifty dollars, please?" I said.

She shrank back. "*Fifty dollars?* Are you out of your mind?"

"Look at this, Aunt Ruth, and you might reconsider," I said, handing her the purchase and sale agreement for our house. "*This* was what I was doing at Crutchley—renegotiating the price."

Aunt Ruth moved her lips slightly as she read. I could see when she reached the purchase price of 200 million dollars. She looked puzzled for a moment. Then she read it again. Then she pulled at her lip and looked suspiciously up at me. "Is this a joke or what?" she said.

I bent over her shoulder and pointed at the paper. "See? Crutchley signed it already. All you have to do is sign it. Aren't you going to thank me for getting the price up there? And *now* can I have fifty dollars for the taxi, please?"

"Two hundred million dollars?" Aunt Ruth whispered.

"Wait a minute!" I pulled it away from her. "You can't

sign it until you sign a promise to let Uncle Marco control his own annuity—and give me fifty for the taxi."

She was out of her chair in a flash. I'd never seen her move so fast. She waddled for her purse and pawed through it and came up with a pen and two twenties and a ten. I smiled sweetly at her as I took the money. "Thank you. And his annuity?"

She waved the pen at me. "He can have it. I couldn't care less now. I'll sign anything you want about it." She peered more closely at me. "How on earth did you do this, Anne?"

"You'll see in a minute. It's in the taxi." I raced to the telephone table, grabbed a piece of notepaper and a pen, and wrote: "From this date onward, Marco Levi will be in control of his annuity, and I have no legal power over it whatsoever." I dated it and thrust it at her. "Sign right here, please," I said.

She scribbled her signature.

I grabbed the paper, folded it, and put it carefully into my coat pocket. "Thank you. Be right back. Leave the door open for us, please." I gave her back the purchase and sale agreement.

I whistled on my way to the taxi. Of course, Aunt Ruth didn't realize that Crutchley would never come up with the money; he'd go bankrupt for sure. Legally committing himself to pay 800 million dollars for seven houses, most of them worth less than a hundred thousand, would be the end of him. Aunt Ruth right now thought we were the only ones with a purchase and sale agreement like this. Until she found out, she'd do anything I wanted.

Henry and I struggled up the walk with the clock and through the open door. We set it down on one of the window seats in the front hall to rest for a minute, just as Uncle Marco came down the stairs, his eyes on me, then Henry.

"Uncle Marco!" I cried, pretending for Aunt Ruth that I hadn't just seen him. We hugged each other. "Good news, Uncle Marco," I said, pulling away. "Aunt Ruth signed the control of the annuity over to you." I turned to her. "Right, Aunt Ruth?"

"I sure did," Aunt Ruth said, looking curiously at the clock, still holding the agreement, not bothering to say hello to Henry. "I'll even increase it if the man wants."

Uncle Marco glanced at me, but he knew Aunt Ruth well enough not to ask any questions in front of her. He looked back at Henry. Henry was watching Uncle Marco, too.

"What *is* this thing, Anne?" Aunt Ruth said. "Where did it come from? What does it have to do with the two hundred million for the house?"

Uncle Marco looked at me. He managed to keep his face blank.

"It's something Crutchley really wanted," I told her. "We let him use it for a while. He thought it could make him the richest developer in the world. That's why it was worth so much to him."

"What are you talking about?" Aunt Ruth nervously lit a

cigarette. “Where did you get this thing, anyway? You still haven't told me what it is.” Smoke poured out of her mouth as she talked.

“It's a special clock, Aunt Ruth. I'll tell you what I can later. Right now we've got to get it down to the basement.” I looked at Henry, then back to her. “I think you better sign that purchase and sale agreement right away, before Crutchley and Company get here. Be sure to point out to him that it's a legal document and he signed it already.”

“Well, *I'm* not going down to the basement,” Aunt Ruth said uncomfortably. “Yes. Have to sign this.” She hurried to-ward the dining room table with the agreement and her pen.

“Will you help us carry this down, Uncle Marco?”

“Let's go,” he said.

CHAPTER NINETEEN

"What did they build in the root cellar?" Uncle Marco asked on the way down.

"It's like . . . a palace," I said. "Uncle Marco, I'm really sorry I—"

He didn't even wait to hear my apology. "Let's leave the clock in the main room for a few minutes before we bring it in to them," he said.

"Why? They really want it."

"Because we have to talk first before . . . before we let them get together."

What would happen when we put the clock together with the creatures? I didn't want to lose it again. We set the clock down on the floor in the main basement room. Then the three of us stood up and looked around at each other.

"Uncle Marco, this is Henry. He's my best friend and I wouldn't have gotten through a minute of this without him. Henry, Uncle Marco. You've heard about him already."

They shook hands, grinning at each other.

"Of course I know who Henry is," Uncle Marco said. "I've spent a great deal of real time sitting on his roof—though it wasn't much time to me."

"But why, Uncle Marco?" I asked him. "Can you tell us now?"

"Yeah. I'm really curious," Henry said.

"First you tell me what's going on with this developer—and how you got Ruth under your thumb in less than a week."

I explained. Uncle Marco was laughing before I finished. He hugged me again. "Wonderful, Annie! And you went to all the trouble to bring the clock back, too. That's important. You've proved yourself now. This time you're coming with me."

"Wait a minute, Uncle Marco," I said. Normally there was no point in asking him direct questions because he was so secretive. But now, with the creatures and the clock depending on me, I wasn't going to let him get away with that. I would get an answer no matter what. "Did you leave the boxes here on purpose? Did you want me to open them?"

And suddenly I realized what the boxes had given me. Not just a way of saving the neighborhood. Something more important—they made me part of the three-in-one.

Uncle Marco looked at me silently.

I crossed my arms, meeting his eyes. "I'm not moving or saying another word until you give me a complete answer," I said.

"Wow. You *have* changed," he said softly.

"Please, Uncle Marco. I'm waiting."

He sighed and shifted from one foot to another. He pushed his hair back and looked away from me. "You never know exactly why you do something, Annie," he said slowly. "And you never know exactly what the result will be. Your opening the boxes was one possibility. I couldn't know what would happen after that. Leaving them here was a chance I took. If you didn't open them, nothing would happen—and maybe the neighborhood would be destroyed. If you did open them and couldn't handle it, then a whole lot of other things could have gone really, really wrong." He looked back at me and shrugged, lifting his arms. "And it turned out—you opened them and did everything exactly right! You saved the neighborhood and you grew up. My gamble—my trust in you—paid off." He waited. "Is that enough of an answer? Are you going to come with me this time?"

"Where? To sit frozen on Henry's roof?" I asked him, still pondering what he had just told me. I was beginning to think I ought to feel proud of myself.

"That's not where I go all the time I'm away—only about a quarter of the time."

"But why do you do that at all?"

"It's very peaceful, sitting there and watching the blur of night and day." He smiled at us. "It's my way of meditating. It's especially interesting when the seasons change. It also makes life more exciting."

"Exciting?" I said skeptically.

"Yes!" he cried, radiating enthusiasm now. "You're not waiting around in real time for things to gradually happen. You're jumping into the future. Fifteen minutes there and fifteen weeks have gone by. Not to mention, it keeps you young. Every time I spend fifteen weeks there, I age only fifteen minutes because that's all the time that goes by for me. It's the opposite when you make a general slowdown of the world. Then you're aging faster than everybody else. That's why you have to watch how many slowdowns you make."

"Oh, wow," Henry breathed. "Because more time goes by for you than for the people in the slowdown."

"You got it," Uncle Marco said.

I was beginning to understand it, too. And I was still feeling really good about myself.

I looked at Henry and back to Uncle Marco. "Maybe you

can explain something we can't figure out. I know why I didn't get stuck in the slowdowns—I'm the nervous system between the creatures and the clock. The clock needs the creatures and the creatures need the clock. They make each other complete, right?"

"That's called a symbiotic relationship," Henry said. Uncle Marco looked impressed.

"Whatever," I said. "I'm part of them, and that keeps me out of the slowdowns. And you have your own clock, Uncle Marco, so you're in control of yourself. But what about Henry? How come he didn't slow down like the rest of the world?"

Henry and Uncle Marco weren't looking at me now; they gazed at each other. "Henry. Think about that vine you've always had in your room," Uncle Marco said.

"Yeah?" Henry said, knitting his brow. "It's just always been there. Nobody ever thought of getting rid of it. It's like . . . part of the house."

"Right. Does it remind you of anything now?" Uncle Marco asked him.

"Maybe." Henry thought about it, frowning. "Something . . . painful, now that I think about it." Absently, he touched the spot on his cheek the clock tendril had made. Then he looked at his finger, his eyes widening. "That's it!" he said. "It looks like one of those root things inside the clock!"

"It's the root stem of my clock, which lives on your roof,"

Uncle Marco said. "That's what happens when you leave an active clock in one place for a while—it digs in and becomes a permanent part of it. And vice versa. You grew up spending every night of your life sleeping next to the essence of the clock. Naturally you became part of it."

"But why did you pick Henry's house?" I asked.

"Best view—the highest spot around. And I just happen to like that house. Always have."

I looked at Henry, shaking my head. "It's kind of hard, taking all this in."

"That's for sure," Henry said.

Uncle Marco laughed. "Well, if things go the way I hope, be prepared to take in a lot more, a lot faster."

"Huh?" Henry and I said.

"You opened the boxes—and you handled it beautifully," Uncle Marco said. "But I'm glad you didn't break the other rule—which was to keep the two boxes apart. I didn't want to miss what might happen when we bring them together. We can move the clock in there now—and if it goes well, then we can get going ourselves, Annie."

"Get going where?"

"My next destination: a surprise. And *not* Henry's roof."

"Uncle Marco," I said slowly. "Can . . . can Henry come, too?" A week ago I never would have imagined asking this; I would have wanted to be alone with Uncle Marco. Now I didn't want to go unless Henry came along. The boxes had made us friends.

Uncle Marco turned to Henry, grinning. "You want to? That's great, Henry!"

Henry looked confused. "Well, I know Annie hinted that you were always going on these mysterious adventures. It sounds interesting, but, I mean, what about my parents? What about school? What about staying around and watching Crutchley lose everything?"

"Yeah? What about watching that?" I said eagerly.

"You don't understand," Uncle Marco said. "If this works, we won't be taking a plane. In a sense, we won't even be leaving this house. I think this is just a short trip. No one will know you were even gone—if nothing goes wrong, that is. Let's bring the clock in and then you can decide."

"But we still don't know what . . . the boxes are *for*," I said, grunting as we lugged the clock across the basement.

"Just think about how they helped you change so many things. And now—watch," said Uncle Marco.

The creatures were expecting us, standing at attention in the colonnades, their heads facing the doorway. When we entered with the clock, they didn't just bow; they prostrated themselves completely, their bodies stretched out on the floor, quivering. The sensation they projected of awe and wonder and devotion to the ends of the earth was so powerful I almost put down the clock and fell to the floor myself.

They weren't just directing their feelings at the clock. I was part of it, too. I had never felt so needed or wanted or appreciated in my life. Tears sprang to my eyes. I was so glad I had done what they asked and brought the clock to them.

One of the creatures stood up and greeted me politely. *Very good, nervous system. It is not too late. Now you must tell the Lord we are all three together at the palace and ask it what to do.*

"Could you hear that, Uncle Marco?" I asked him.

He nodded.

"I could, too," Henry said.

"Good. We'll be able to do this together, if we ever have to."

I looked down at the clock. I bowed. *We are here at the palace. Your worshipers—who are devoted to you forever—want to know what to do next.*

For a change, the clock didn't make me wait. I remembered how it had obeyed my thought to lash out at Crutchley, back in his office. Had I proved myself to the clock, too? The dial clicked—and stopped on a mark like an upside-down U. I conveyed this to the creatures.

A silent cheer rose around us. The creatures were dancing and radiating more waves of pleasure. *Put the Lord into the archway! Hurry!*

Uncle Marco was studying the palace. "Good. They did well. It should be a nice fit," he said.

We set the clock down in front of the large arched opening in the middle of the first three levels of the palace. The creatures all turned so that they were prostrating themselves in its direction.

"Now I think all we need to do is just give it a little push," Uncle Marco said. All three of us pushed the clock right into the opening; it fit snugly inside.

And kept on going, slowly at first, then faster and faster. It looked as though it were sliding down a steep, slippery slope, getting smaller with distance—except there was no slope there, just the cement basement floor and the stone wall directly behind the palace. But the clock didn't seem to be aware of the floor or the wall. It was going past them or around them or somehow through them, into some kind of space that hadn't been there before.

Uncle Marco was enthralled, beaming, his hands clasped together. "I've always wanted to see this!" he whispered. "Watch! Don't take your eyes away for a second."

"But where did it *go*?" I wailed. "I just got it back—and now it's gone!"

"Not if you go with it," Uncle Marco said, glancing toward me, then back again.

Because now the creatures were running, swarming. And, true to form, the big, sleek ones were in the lead, the small, spotty ones in back. They followed the clock, slipping and sliding down the impossible, nonexistent incline—the exit that wouldn't have been there at all if the palace had not been built and the clock had not entered it.

Nervous system! Nervous system! Come! We need you. We can't make it without youououououou!

I was chewing on my lip. What was happening? Did they actually want me to come with them?

As they grew smaller with distance, the palace began to glow, the filaments becoming shimmering silver.

"Come on," Uncle Marco said, getting to his hands and knees and approaching the opening.

"You're going in there?" I said, terrified.

Upstairs, in another world, the doorbell rang.

Henry and I turned to each other. "Crutchley!" we both said. And I knew Henry wanted as much as I did to watch Crutchley take the news of his collapse.

"You can find out about that when we come back," Uncle Marco said, now almost entirely inside the opening. "This door, this portal, won't last long. If you don't come now, you'll never have the chance again." He turned back to us, already shrinking into the distance. "Come on!" he cried, his voice echoing slightly.

"But where are you going? What's in there?" I called out to him. It was awful, having him come back and then disappear so soon.

"You have to take risks in life!" he called back, his voice fading as he shrank into the distance. "They need you!"

"Why can't he ever give a straight answer?" I wailed.

Henry and I looked at each other in confusion. It must have been more difficult for him because he had never met Uncle Marco before and, for all he knew, he could be nuts.

Still, we had seen what we had seen. And this was our only chance to go.

"Well?" Henry asked me.

"I don't know!" I cried out. "But . . . I'm part of it now, part of the clock and the creatures. They need me. And without them, we would never have beaten Crutchley."

The palace was shining more brightly now and also trembling, like a reflection of lights in a pond at night that could instantly dissolve.

". . . in the basement. I never go down there," a voice brayed from above. We heard footsteps on the stairs.

"Aunt Ruth and Crutchley!" I whispered. "They can't see this!"

Henry took my hand. "I'll be right behind you," he said. "I won't let go."

We got to our knees. There was no room to enter side by side, but Henry, behind me, had a good grip on my hand. I crawled in, one-handed.

And then there was nothing but the shimmering around us, and the sudden unexpected depth in front of us, and the sensation of slowly falling, like flying in a dream.

William Sleator is the best-selling author of *Interstellar Pig*, *The Night the Heads Came*, *The Beasties*, and many other popular chilling novels. Hailed by R. L. Stine as "one of my favorite young adult writers," Mr. Sleator divides his time between Boston, Massachusetts, and rural Thailand.